LOVE TO PROVE YOU WRONG

OLD PINE COVE #2

by

SOPHIE-LEIGH ROBBINS

Love to Prove You Wrong

Cover design by Joey Van Olden
Editing by Serena Clarke

If my book boyfriends give you heart palpitations, please consult a doctor (or call your best friend to swoon over him together).

To my best friends.
You mean the world to me!
(PS: Don't drop this book in your bathtub)

CONTENTS

CHAPTER ONE

"There's a duck in the lobby. A living, quacking duck!"

Uh-oh. Not this again.

Diane's panicked voice reached the reception area of the Old Pine Cove Inn moments before she came bursting in. I plastered on my biggest smile and waited for the rest of her tirade.

She threw her hands in the air while pinning Carter and me down with an ominous look. "Well, you heard me. Don't just stand there like idiots. Do something."

"There's no need to panic. It's a duck, not a lion," Carter said, not looking up from the list of guest reservations he was checking.

Diane rubbed her temples with her well-manicured fingers. A big sigh escaped her mouth as she shook her head. It reminded me of the kind of sigh my cousin utters when her toddler insists on having his sandwich cut into squares, then refuses to eat it.

"I don't care what it is. Animals don't belong inside an inn. It's unsanitary. If this duck doesn't get removed from the premises soon, I can't have Asher's wedding here. What if everyone contracts some nasty disease? We've got seventy people coming from out of town. Seventy!"

"I promise you it won't happen again. I apologize, and so does Duckota," I said.

I stepped away from the front desk and made my way to the lobby where Duckota was frolicking around like the happy duck she was.

"It has a name?" Diane's raised eyebrow told me how ridiculous she thought it was to name a duck.

"She sure does," I said and threw her a weak smile. What was wrong with naming an animal? Dogs and cats got named by their owners. There was no reason ducks should be left behind.

I crouched down behind one of the lounge chairs to get to Duckota's hiding place. She probably took shelter in the secluded spot after hearing Diane's panicked screams. I couldn't blame Duckota, though. Anyone would be scared of Diane when they heard her throw one of her famous tantrums. In fact, I was scared of her myself from time to time.

After a mere ten seconds of chasing Duckota, I got a hold of her. "There. She won't escape anytime soon, I promise."

Diane gave me a curt nod before returning her attention to Lilian, the wedding planner. At least now that Duckota was being removed from the lobby, Diane wouldn't have anything to complain about anymore.

"Addy dear, just a minor remark."

Okay, maybe there was something else. I should've known.

I turned around to face Diane, the duck getting restless in my hands.

"Yes?"

The old lady pointed to the framed photographs of my dad and me that I'd hung above the fireplace. "Those pictures will have to go. No one wants to look at someone else's family photos at a wedding."

"Sure, no problem," I said with a smile, even though I could feel my jaw tightening. I probably shouldn't have let her rearrange the inn's interior, but this wedding was too important to argue over small details.

Right on cue, Duckota started quacking. I rushed her outside to put her back in the fenced area I had built for her in the backyard. It was nothing fancy, but it did the trick. Or at least, it was supposed to. I couldn't figure out how she managed to escape every day. When I'd found her near the fountain in the town square a few weeks earlier, I saw her wing was injured. The vet had told me the duck would never be able to fly again, yet somehow, she kept finding a way out of her enclosure.

Unfortunately, the commotion after running into Diane

had been a bit too much for my sweet duck. As soon as she was back outside, she pooped in my hands. Great, just what I needed.

I wiped my hands on a patch of grass.

"Now listen to me carefully, Duckota. No more escaping. We don't want to lose our best customer, now do we?" I said while snapping the lock shut.

Gosh, now I was talking to a duck? Maybe I needed to get out more. That was easier said than done, though. Between running the inn and managing employees, there was hardly any time left to go out and mingle. Let alone mingle and find a boyfriend.

I got back inside, making a beeline for the employees' bathroom. After a royal amount of soap and water, I got the duck poop and its accompanying smell off my hands.

When I joined Carter at the reception desk, I threw him a look. "Was it really necessary to tell Diane not to panic? You could've just reassured her that we would take care of the duck."

He shrugged. "It's a duck, Addy. None of the other guests have complained about having Duckota around. In fact, they all love her."

"I'm aware of that, but you know what Diane's like."

"A control freak?"

"Well, yeah. She likes to have it her way. And don't forget that her grandson's wedding is going to bring in a lot of money for the inn. Please stop taunting her like that. Besides, she's right about Duckota. She shouldn't be in here, but I don't know how I can prevent her from escaping all the time."

Carter looked up from his paperwork and grinned. "If she keeps it up, you might have to start charging her."

"That won't be necessary, thank goodness. I have high hopes for buying the patch of land next door. As soon as this wedding is over, I'll have all the funds I need to put my name on the title deed. Duckota will be one happy duck when that happens."

Ever since Dad left the management of the inn in my hands, I had dreamt of adding a petting zoo to the place. It would have alpacas, rabbits, chickens, goats, and ducks. Maybe even a pig or a pony. I'd already gotten a lot of positive comments from guests when I talked to them about my ideas. All I needed were the funds to buy an extra patch of land. Hosting Asher's wedding here would seal the deal – if we kept his grandmother happy, of course. Diane was known for her strong opinions and high maintenance behavior, but I knew how to handle her.

Four more weeks of catering to her needs and fulfilling her requests. Four more weeks of her getting on my nerves. Four more weeks of her trying to rearrange the interior.

I let my gaze wander through the lobby, wondering why Diane wanted to tweak the look of the inn. Almost every review I got online mentioned the charming atmosphere of the place, something I was extremely proud of. The mahogany floors gave the seating area next to the lobby a rustic feel. In the winter months, the fireplace roared daily and the comfortable armchairs offered guests a cozy place to read a book.

The wooden stairs leading to the guest rooms often creaked with every step, but those sounds only added to the charm in my opinion. And I absolutely adored the mountain view our dining room offered. No matter the season, the scenery outside was never short of spectacular.

"Addy?" Carter asked, pulling me out of my thoughts.

"Yes?"

He shoved a piece of paper toward me. "We received a last-minute reservation request last night. Can I allocate room 3E to this guest, or should we keep that open for emergencies?"

I shoved the paper back into his direction without giving it a glance. "Of course you can. What emergency would we keep it for? The Queen of England coming to visit Old Pine Cove?"

Carter shrugged. "Just wanted to double-check. I don't want to make any mistakes."

"I love that you do that, but how long have you been working here now? Five months? I trust you, Carter. You don't have to double-check everything with me."

He nodded, then opened the online reservation manager. "Kermit the Frog is all confirmed."

"Who is what now?" I asked.

Carter pointed to the screen. "Kermit the Frog. Says so right here."

I raised one of my eyebrows and let out a laugh. "Kermit the Frog is going to stay at the Old Pine Cove Inn?"

"Well, I'm assuming that's not his real name. Maybe it's

one of those tactics celebrities use to protect their identity."

"Oh, okay," I said. "As long as he's not a serial killer and he has a valid credit card, I'm fine with whatever name this guest uses. I'm going to catch up on some paperwork. Would you mind running to the kitchen and checking up on Alex? He wanted to go over this week's menu with one of us."

"Sure. Got any pointers?"

"As long as he doesn't want to serve duck, it's all good," I said.

Carter laughed. "Great. Oh, and thanks for trusting me. I appreciate it."

As Carter disappeared into the kitchen, I couldn't help but smile as well. The kid was a blessing to have around. Even though he was only twenty-two and had a knack for taunting Diane, he had a great work ethic and never complained when I asked him to do something. Plus, guests loved him. Hiring him had cut into my budget, but the inn was growing so much that I couldn't keep doing all the work by myself anymore. There was only so much time in a day.

I printed out some paperwork and stapled it together before retreating into my office. It was small but cozy. Right after I became the new manager of the inn, I'd taken down the hideous brown wallpaper and replaced it with two coats of white paint. I'd also opted for one teal-colored wall. A splash of color had never hurt anyone.

There was just enough space to open the door without

hitting the desk, and the tiny window gave me a stunning, albeit restricted, view of the mountains. In winter, they were completely covered in snow, but in spring, the lower slopes were blooming. I loved seeing all those beautiful flowers pop up between the pine trees.

I slid into my chair and started working on an occupancy rate report that I could use to check our marketing ROI. A mere ten minutes later, someone rang the bell at the reception desk. If it was about the duck again, I'd scream.

I slid my chair back, but when I got out of my office, there was no one to be seen.

"Hello?" I called out.

"Just a minute."

A man was crouched down on the floor at the reception desk, going through his suitcase.

"Here it is." The crouching male got up and slapped his printed reservation on the counter.

When his eyes met mine, my breath got stuck in my throat. He narrowed his eyes, as if he wanted to zoom in on my face. Then his eyes grew wide, and a puff of air left his mouth.

"Fat… I mean, Addy?" he asked.

Oh. My. Word. Did he almost call me Fat Addy? It had been years since I'd heard that disgusting nickname. A nickname *he* had made viral in high school after watching that movie *Pitch Perfect.*

I rolled my eyes at him. "Justin Miller. I'd say it's a pleasure, but it really isn't."

He cocked an eyebrow and paired his gaze with a smirk

I wanted to slap off his face. "Is that how you talk to all of your guests?"

"Of course not, only the ones I don't like. You're the first one so far, if you must know."

Then it dawned on me. He was staying here. For real. At my inn. I mean, he had a suitcase with him and a printed reservation. It was obvious what his plans were.

"Well, are you going to check me in or what?"

I crossed my arms over my chest. "We're all out of rooms. I'm sorry. There was a double reservation."

Instead of leaving, he laughed. "I don't think so. The confirmation for this reservation came through this morning."

I snatched his reservation from the counter. "Kermit the Frog? Really? I see you haven't changed one bit."

"What? I love that guy. And I don't want everyone to know I'm back. At least not yet anyway."

A rush of panic coursed through me. He wasn't going to stick around for long, was he?

"Back? What are you doing here, Justin? I thought you had moved. Forever."

He grinned at me. "Asher's wedding, of course. What person would let his best friend get married without his oldest friend there to witness the entire thing? Maybe get up to some mischief before he ties the knot?"

"The wedding's not until next month," I said.

He nodded. "That's right."

"You're staying here for four weeks?"

"I am," he said, handing me a platinum American Express card.

"Don't you have to work? And can't you stay with family?"

He leaned on the counter. "I'm in between projects. And yes, I could stay with family, but I don't want to." He scrunched his nose as if I had asked him if he wanted a complimentary platter of duck poop delivered to his room.

There was nothing I could do but check him in. If he wanted to stay here, I couldn't exactly refuse to, unless I wanted to get entangled in a nasty lawsuit.

I handed him his credit card back, together with the keys to his room. "Your room is located on the third floor. Enjoy your stay."

"Oh, I sure will," he said with a smile before walking away.

I rolled my eyes again. He hadn't changed one bit. Sure, he looked even hotter than he had back in high school, but what did looks matter if you were rotten inside?

"Was that Justin Miller, or do I need glasses?" Suzie, my best friend, whom I met two years ago, asked. She was standing right next to the front door, a big box of books in her arms.

"Let me help you with those," I said, ignoring her question.

I took the box from her and put it in my office. Suzie ran the local bookstore and provided guests of the inn with books at great prices. The order forms flew out the door every week. The reviews we got on travel websites almost always mentioned the unique service, something I was extremely proud of. Granted, it was Suzie who had come up with the idea of "Books in Bed", but the execution had been a team effort.

"Well?" she asked, leaning on my desk.

I turned around and riffled through a drawer of paperwork. I didn't want Suzie to see my shaking hands while I talked to her.

"How come you know Justin Miller?" I asked. "You only moved back here a couple of months ago, and he was long gone by then. Thank goodness."

Suzie walked over to my side of the desk and shoved her phone under my nose. "Um, hello. Justin Miller, star of the hit series *In Dire Need*, not to mention a ton of successful rom-com movies. Who doesn't know the guy?"

I snatched the phone from her hands and peered at the pictures Google had pulled up for her. "Huh."

Unfortunately, she didn't stop questioning me. "Come on, Addy, you have to tell me more than *huh*."

I let out a sigh as I closed the door of the office. I wanted no one to hear what I was about to tell Suzie.

"Remember how I told you about that guy who used to call me Fat Addy in high school? And then everyone started calling me that? Well, he and Justin Miller are the same guy."

Suzie gasped. "No way."

"Him laughing at my expense every chance he got drove guys away from me. He was the town stud and everyone looked up to him, even though they didn't always agree with his behavior."

"What is he doing here?" Suzie asked. "And at the inn of all places?"

"He and Asher are best friends. He came back here for the wedding."

"I see," she said, then narrowed her eyes. "And Asher? Do we still like him? Or should we hate him as well?"

I shook my head. "Asher has never been rude to me. He never spurred Justin on either. If anything, he tried to get Justin to tone it down with the nicknaming. Not that it helped."

Suzie smiled at me. "Let's just hope he stays out of your hair and that he won't cause any trouble."

I laughed. "Justin Miller *is* trouble, believe me."

Three taps on the door cut our conversation short. I knew it was Carter, as I'd been the one to suggest he use a special knock so that I would immediately know it was him and not some random guest.

"Well, duty calls. But I'll see you tomorrow for the Spring Picnic meeting, right?" I asked.

Suzie nodded. "Alex and I will be there. I told him he'd have to go home alone, though. We're still on for that girls' night out we talked about, right?"

"Definitely."

"Great, I'll see you tomorrow," Suzie said.

She waved me goodbye, and I joined Carter at the reception desk where a demanding guest had almost brought the guy to tears. After resolving the issue and finishing the occupancy report, I closed the reception desk for the night and headed home. It was a good thing I hadn't run into

Justin again. How I was going to cope with him around for an entire month, I had no clue, but I did know I had to find a way to stay as far away from him as possible.

As soon as I closed the door of my house behind me, I went into my bedroom and changed into loungewear. My place was located right beside the inn so I could be there in a matter of minutes, if I needed to. It was still secluded enough that I could shut out the world as well. If I didn't, then I'd be catering to guests well into the night. There was always something or someone needing my attention, but I was only human after all.

The house only had one bedroom, a tiny bathroom and a small garden, but since I was single, it was perfect for me.

I settled myself on the couch with the latest copy of *Farm Weekly*, but I couldn't stay focused on the article about alpaca grooming, nor the one about the best way to grow your own tomatoes. My thoughts kept wandering after every sentence I read, zooming in on Justin. Why did I care about him being here? And why did his arrival feel like such a shock? High school was a long time ago.

I chucked the magazine aside and turned on Netflix, pulling up *In Dire Need*. If Justin was the star Suzie claimed he was, I had to check it out.

Of course, I'd heard people talk about *In Dire Need* before, but I had always assumed it was some stupid show that only aired on one of those obscure channels. Townspeople here often got excited about things that were completely mundane.

So yeah, I had never realized how popular the series

was. I hardly had time to watch TV or go to the movies. I mostly played old nineties series in the background while catching up on housework. If I didn't, the loneliness had a way of creeping up on me and taking me by surprise. Kind of like Justin Miller.

I pushed play on the first episode, half expecting it to suck. But when Netflix asked me if I was still watching *In Dire Need,* it dawned on me that hours had passed since I'd so much as moved.

I rolled my neck from side to side, trying to ease the cramps that had appeared from sitting in the same position for hours.

Nothing about his performance made sense to me. In the series, Justin came across as the sweetest, sexiest specimen alive. Seeing his character on screen even made my heart pound a little faster. Yet in real life, he was a jerk.

I turned off the TV and stared into the dark. Why had I even watched an entire season of that show?

As I slid under the covers, I couldn't get Justin out of my head. Or at least, his character Gabriel Finch. He was a great actor; I'd give him that. But there was no way in hell I'd ever admit that to him.

CHAPTER TWO

"Admit it, you loved it."

"*Loved* is a strong word. But yeah, maybe I liked it a little bit. It's a good show."

"Ha, I knew it. How many episodes did you watch?" Suzie asked while ringing up the magazine I'd picked up at her bookstore, Got It Covered.

"A couple," I said.

I didn't want to lie to my best friend, but I wasn't planning on admitting I was hooked on Justin's show. I had even eaten my lunch at home just so I could catch an extra episode of *In Dire Need*.

Suzie leaned her elbows on the counter, resting her head in her hands. "He plays such a dreamy guy, right?"

I shrugged as if I couldn't care less. "It doesn't change

my opinion about the real him, though. He might be Gabriel Finch to the world, but to me, he's still Justin Miller – immature and, and…"

Suzie cocked an eyebrow. "And hot?"

A laugh escaped my mouth. "Stop it, Suzie. I was going to say that he's immature and a clown. He booked his reservation under Kermit the Frog, for crying out loud. What grown man would do that?"

"Maybe someone exactly like him? You know, a celebrity?"

I put the magazine under my arm and shook my head. "Being the lead in a popular TV series and acting in a few movies doesn't make him a celebrity."

Suzie put her hand on her hip. "Addy, the guy's got one and a half million followers on Instagram. That's pretty famous in my book."

"He does?"

I got my phone out and looked him up. She was right. It was staring me right in the face. Justin Miller. One point five million followers. He probably had millions of followers on other platforms as well. Figures.

"How could I have missed this?" I asked, more to myself than anything.

I scrolled down to peek at his pictures. In every one of them, he was looking right into the camera, his smile as deep as his dimples. Beach days, hip restaurant outings, movie premieres… His world was the opposite of mine. For me, a typical Friday night involved defrosting a pizza while catching up on laundry; his was a mix of Pinterest-worthy parties and fancy food.

I couldn't help but laugh at the thought of him being back in Old Pine Cove, where nothing exciting ever happened.

"What's so funny?"

"Nothing," I said. "Justin's in for a culture shock now that he's back. I bet you he'll get bored of this town in a matter of days."

"Maybe it's a welcome change of scenery for him. Life in L.A. can get pretty hectic. Trust me, I'm speaking from experience."

She really was. Before moving to Old Pine Cove, Suzie used to live in Los Angeles. But I was happy and grateful she'd decided to move to Old Pine Cove after reconnecting with Alex, the love of her life. If she hadn't, we'd never have grown so close.

I bit my lip. "Maybe. But you know what? I shouldn't care about any of it. It's his life. He's just a guest, nothing more. And I'll make sure to treat him that way. You know, like a professional inn owner."

Suzie smiled at me, a twinkle in her eye. "Just a guest, huh? And yet you can't seem to stop talking about him."

I waved her remark away. I could stop talking about him if I wanted to. Sure, he'd been the first thing on my mind when I woke up that morning, but that was to be expected. I had binge-watched his show the night before, and he had gotten on my nerves with the whole immature Kermit the Frog thing. That's all it was. It had nothing to do with his dimples or his smile. Absolutely nothing.

"Are you going to follow him?" Suzie asked, motioning to my phone.

I closed the app. "Of course not. I don't care about seeing his pictures in my feed every day."

Why would I follow him? He'd be notified of it, and the last thing I wanted was him thinking I was interested in his life. Checking his profile occasionally without actually following him would be a much smarter move.

"Four weeks from now, you can forget all about him again," Suzie said, throwing me an encouraging smile.

"And it won't be a moment too soon."

As I drove back to the inn, I went over my to-do list in my head. We were opening ten new rooms at the end of next week and I still needed to finalize the bedding. Every room was going to have a flower theme and name. Lily. Daisy. Begonia. Reservations for the themed rooms were already pouring in, so I was positive that it was a good move.

When I pulled into my parking spot at the inn, my mood shifted. Diane stood on the porch, arms crossed, her face bright red.

I took three deep breaths before exiting the car.

"Hi, Diane," I said in the most cheerful voice I could muster.

"Addison, this has got to stop. I'm serious."

"Why? What happened?" I asked, even though I had my suspicions.

"That duck happened." She spoke the words between closed teeth. If her eyes could've stabbed me, I'd be on my way to the hospital.

"Duckota escaped again?"

Diane laughed hysterically. "Of course. And then she did a number two on the floor. Do you think that's normal, Addison?"

Did I think it was normal that ducks pooped? Yeah, I did. Okay, maybe not inside. But Duckota was an animal. I couldn't exactly send her to her room to think about what she'd done.

"You know what, I'll take care of it right away," I said.

Diane tapped her foot on the ground. "You told me yesterday this wouldn't happen again. You promised me."

I swallowed down the lump forming in my throat. Four more weeks, I repeated to myself. Four. Long. Weeks. "You're right, I did promise. I'll make sure to take extra precautions this time. And I'd love to offer you a lunch, on the house. Alex is making risotto."

She hesitated for a moment, then lowered her arms. "Fine. I'll accept your offer, but that doesn't mean I'm happy with what happened."

"Okay," I said with a squeaky voice before rushing inside.

I could hear Duckota's quacking coming from behind the reception desk. I took slow, deliberate steps so I wouldn't scare her off. "Come here, girl. It's okay. No need to be afraid."

Carter appeared next to me, a bucket and sponge in his hands. "I cleaned up the mess she made before someone could step in it."

"You're a lifesaver, thanks."

Carter put a hand on my arm. "No worries. Things got pretty nasty in here with Diane having one of her drama queen attacks."

"Shh, not so loud. She might hear you."

Carter shifted the weight from his left foot to his right, almost as if he was afraid to speak. "You know, you could tell her that you're the boss."

I blinked. "I am the boss."

He threw his hands in the air. "Then why do you let Diane get away with acting like she runs the place? No offense," he added.

Deep down, I knew he was right, but I needed to keep her happy. No matter how much of a nuisance she could be, she did choose the inn to host a wedding. And the client was king. Or in this case, queen.

"I agree that she's demanding," I told Carter, "but in four weeks she'll be out of our hair. I'm sure we can cope with her fits as long as Duckota here stays put."

With one swift motion, I got ahold of the duck, then I transported her outside, this time putting a paper cloth between her and my hands. Better safe than sorry.

I once again clicked the lock in place, although I had my doubts about its efficiency. Seven times the duck had escaped this week, and it was only Wednesday.

"You need a higher fence, or this will keep happening."

I rolled my eyes. Him again. I turned around, hand on my hip.

"Tell me something new."

Justin grinned at me. "If you want, I can help you stop this duck from escaping."

"Help? Why would you suddenly want to help me? If only you had that attitude in high school. It could've made my life a whole lot easier."

He ran a hand through his hair, but the thick strands fell right back in front of his eyes. "We're not in high school anymore, Addy. When are you going to let it go? It's in the past."

I crossed my arms. "That's easy for you to say. You were nothing but rude to me, Justin. I had to listen to everyone calling me Fat Addy for two years."

"You're right, I shouldn't have called you that. But in my defense, I was a clueless sixteen-year-old boy. I mean, being immature and inconsiderate is kind of normal at that age."

"So you admit it? That you were wrong?"

He held his hands up in the air. "Yes, officer, I do."

"Don't get cheeky with me, mister."

His mouth twitched, and I could tell he was having trouble suppressing a smile. "Mister?"

"This might all seem like fun and games to you, but I have a business to run here. I don't have time for your silly comments."

Justin took a step forward, closing the distance between us. I took a step back and grabbed ahold of the fence. Why was he standing so close to me that I could see the blue around his irises? Was he doing this on purpose, knowing full well he could use his looks and chiseled body to mislead people? To make them feel all confused?

"I know this is serious. That's why I want to help you. Let me make that fence for you."

"Why? What will you get out of it?" I asked in a snappy tone.

Justin raised one of his eyebrows and laughed. "Oh my God, Addy. Nothing, except maybe a friendly word from you. You keep reminding me how bad I was to you when we were teenagers, but you're not so friendly to me now."

I pursed my lips. "Fine. But only because it'll get Diane off my back. And I'll pay you."

"You don't have to pay me. I don't need the money."

I leveled him with a stare. "I am paying you or the deal's off. I don't want to owe you anything. And I don't want any favors either."

He licked his lips. *Wow.* Why did he have to have such a soft-looking mouth?

"Deal. But you'll have to stop checking me out," he said with a grin.

Ugh. The guy made my blood boil.

I pushed him away, which in hindsight was a bad move. Touching his muscled chest only made me weaker in the knees.

"I would never check you out, Justin Miller. And I don't care that you're famous or rich. It doesn't change my opinion about you. Maybe your one and a half million followers think you're *the bomb*, but I know better. I know the real you."

He pinned me in place with a grin. "Oh, do you now?

You can't stand me, but you know exactly how many followers I have? That's not contradictory at all. One might even say that you're obsessed with me."

I narrowed my eyes. "I hate you, Justin."

He chuckled. "Whatever you say, Addy."

Then he turned on his heel, leaving me alone with Duckota. My heart was racing as I watched him walk away. Hating him would've been so much easier if he wasn't so freaking sexy.

CHAPTER THREE

I only just made it in time to attend the town meeting at the community center. I had left Carter in charge of the inn and hoped he wouldn't run into trouble, especially not with Duckota.

I pushed the door to the community center open and stood on my tiptoes to scan the crowd until I spotted Suzie. She waved me over and I took a seat next to her and Alex.

"Sorry I couldn't be here earlier. I have so much going on, it's a miracle I got here on time," I said.

"No worries, we'll catch up after, right?" Suzie asked.

I nodded. "Definitely."

A night out with my best friend was exactly what I needed. Organizing the spring event, not so much, but as a local business owner, I had no choice. People expected everyone who was someone in this town to commit to helping with the organization of seasonal events, including this one. The Spring Picnic was a classic. It was a ton of fun, although I wished I could've skipped my commitment to it for a year. I had enough on my plate with Asher's wedding and Diane breathing down my neck.

Milly, who owned the local bedding store, walked onto the stage at the front of the room and tapped the microphone. The crowd grew silent, and all heads turned to face her.

"Good evening, everyone. I'm excited to see so many faces here tonight," she said. "I would like to—"

The screeching sound of the double doors opening cut her speech short. A couple of gasps went through the room and people started whispering amongst themselves. I shook my head. It didn't surprise me that Justin had to come in late, making a show of his arrival.

"Carry on," he said with a grin.

He walked right up to my row and took the empty seat next to me.

"What are you doing here, Justin?" I whispered.

He shrugged. "It's a town meeting, right? I'm in town, so technically I'm entitled to be here."

"You don't even live here."

"Shh, Milly's talking."

I stared him down. "Did you just shush me?"

A smirk stretched across his face. "What? It's inappropriate to talk when someone is addressing a crowd."

It came as no surprise that someone like Justin would

enjoy trying to get under my skin. The worst part was that he was succeeding in his intentions. My blood was boiling already, and he'd only been here for a minute. I shot him my most annoyed glare, throwing in the stink eye for good measure.

"Shut up, Justin."

He glared at me. "You shut up."

"Is there a problem?" Milly asked.

It took me a few moments and some elbowing from Suzie to realize Milly was talking to me. Fifty heads turned in my direction, making me cringe in my seat. The whispering of other townies didn't bode well either. The fact that Justin and I had been yapping away during the town meeting would dominate the town's gossip before I could blink.

I fabricated a forced smile. "No, not at all. I apologize. I stand by what you were saying."

"So, you agree to be allocated to this task?" Milly asked.

Crap. What was she talking about? I hesitated for a moment, then realized this was about the Spring Picnic. What tasks could be involved that I wouldn't want to be allocated to?

"Sure. Put my name on the list," I said.

I didn't have a clue what I'd just agreed to, but I was positive it was better than admitting I hadn't been paying attention.

"Great," Milly said.

Heat spread to my cheeks. I sank deeper into my chair, wishing the ground would open up and swallow me whole. Why did Justin have a knack for embarrassing me all the time? It was like high school all over again.

I glanced sideways. He sat there looking all yummy, his eyes twinkling with delight. This entire thing was nothing but a joke to him. Then again, why would he even care? To him, these four weeks were a welcome break from real life.

But to me, this *was* my life. Gosh, I should stay as far away from him as possible. I didn't need anyone messing with my life, especially not someone like Justin Miller.

Milly pushed her glasses up her nose then trailed her finger down her list of tasks. "Who wants to help build the food and drink stands for the open-air cinema? Preferably someone who's good with wood."

Justin's hand shot up.

"I'm good with wood," he said with a grin.

I rolled my eyes. "Classy."

"Great. You two will have a wonderful time together." Milly smiled at us and looked at her list again, ready to allocate another task.

I sat up straighter. "Excuse me, Milly. What do you mean *you two*?"

She creased her eyebrows. "You are responsible for the food and drinks for the movie night. Justin's responsible for building the stands so you can actually sell the food and drinks. This can only work if you two work together."

My throat tightened. "I don't know if that's a good idea. Justin doesn't even live here."

It was a lame excuse, but I had to try something to get out of this. Manning the food and drink stands was a fun job, just not with Justin there as well.

He scoffed. "What? Now you're discriminating because I don't currently live here? I want to help. Plus, I lived here for eighteen years. Isn't that what counts?"

I crossed my arms over my chest. "You sure want to help out a lot these days. What's with this Good Samaritan act?"

"Guys, there's no need to fight over this. I'm sure we can rearrange things if working together makes you uncomfortable," Milly said.

I looked up and almost told her that yes, we should rearrange, but Justin cut me short.

"Thank you, but that won't be necessary. We're both adults. We can handle this, can't we, Addy?"

I gritted my teeth. He had me backed into a corner. If I said no now, I would come across as a whiny child. That was not the image I wanted to create for myself.

"Fine. We'll work together."

"I'm glad to hear that," Milly said. "Next one up is quilting some picnic blankets we can auction off. Anyone up for that one? I need three volunteers."

As Milly appointed the quilters, I wondered why Justin was so keen on teaming up with me. It made no sense, but then again, did anything that involved Justin ever make sense? He loved taunting me, that much was clear. Maybe if I didn't show him how much he got to me, he would back off.

I spent the rest of the meeting looking straight ahead. If I glanced at Justin again, I might explode and slap him.

When all the tasks were finally allocated and Milly had

thanked everyone for coming, I heaved a relieved sigh. Everyone swarmed together at the tables in the back where fresh coffee and cake was up for grabs. Justin left to talk to Asher and Layla, Asher's wife-to-be. He was finally out of my hair.

Suzie put a hand on my arm. "Are you okay? You look like a volcano about to burst."

"Yeah, I'm fine. Just a bit shocked that I'll have to team up with Justin."

"I'm sure it'll all work out fine. Besides, there's worse faces to look at all day long," she said, wiggling her eyebrows with a smile.

Alex laughed. "Hey, I heard that."

"Oh, you know I don't have eyes for anyone but you," Suzie said.

She pulled Alex in for a hug and kissed him. They were so adorable together I couldn't help but smile, yet I also felt a tiny bit jealous. The love they shared was something I could only dream of.

"Excuse me, Addison."

I turned around. "Oh, hello, Diane."

I wondered what she wanted to discuss now. At least it couldn't concern Duckota. For the duck to have traveled all the way from the inn to the community center would've been a miracle.

She crossed her arms over her chest. The look on her face terrified me. I didn't know what it was with her, but the woman had a knack for scaring everyone away.

"That Miller boy being here, is that going to be a problem? For the wedding, I mean."

"I don't think so," I said.

That couldn't be further from the truth of what I was really thinking, but Diane didn't need to know that. It would only make her worry, and a worried Diane was ten times worse than a normal one. Not that Diane ever came across as normal.

She nodded in appreciation. "Good. The boy is trouble. I don't want him messing things up."

Why did she assume that I had any say in what he did or didn't do? I wasn't his mother.

"How would he mess things up?" I asked cautiously. "He's Asher's best friend. I doubt he'll do anything to jeopardize his wedding day."

"Maybe not on purpose, but the boy has a bad reputation of getting my Asher into less than charming situations. He's staying at the Old Pine Cove Inn and you're the owner, so it's only fair I'm expecting you to keep an eye on him. Before and during the wedding."

Sure, because that was a totally reasonable request. I would love to spend my days running around and checking up on what my guests were doing in their free time, especially Justin freaking Miller.

"Maybe you can talk to him about your concerns," I said. "I think he'll be more inclined to listen to you than to me."

Diane looked over to the snacks table where Asher and Justin were shoving cake in their mouths, then trying to smile without anything spilling out.

The old lady put a hand on her cheek and shook her head in disbelief. "That scenario right there? That's what I mean. My Asher is never like this. Whenever he's with that Miller boy, he turns into a teenager again."

"I see what you mean," I told her. At least we saw eye to eye on the topic of Justin being a complete baby. That still didn't mean I should act like his mother and keep him in check. That was entirely up to Justin himself.

Alex appeared by our sides. He gently put his hand on Diane's arm, and her entire face lit up. "I'm sorry to interrupt, but would you mind going over the menu for the wedding one more time? I've got a couple of questions about the entrees."

I shot him a thankful smile before walking away. If he hadn't intervened, Diane never would've stopped pressing the issue.

I lowered my voice as I confided in my best friend. "I'm so glad I hired Alex. He's a keeper."

Suzie beamed. "The feeling is definitely mutual. He loves being the new chef at the inn. And such great hours too. He's thrilled that he doesn't have to work past three p.m. So am I. Otherwise, we'd never see each other. Plus, now he can still teach yoga."

"Him getting his chef's degree couldn't have come at a better time. When Rick told me he only wanted to work nights from now on, I panicked at first."

Suzie put a finger on her lips. "What club did he want to be a member of again?"

I giggled. "The official support group for husbands of

crochet addicts."

"I'm one hundred percent sure that's just a fancy name for sharing a couple of beers with other men who want a few hours away from their wives," she said with a chuckle.

"And it all turned out perfect. Rick's got his membership pass, and I have Alex," I said. "Although… Diane isn't causing him too much stress, is she?"

Suzie shook her head. "You know what she's like when he's around. Diane loves Alex."

I glanced over at the pair of them discussing menu options. "I wish she would treat me with the same fondness."

"You do know you can be stricter with her, right?" Suzie asked, the tone of her voice careful.

"I know, but it's Diane. She's hard to please. And I don't want to anger her. Have you seen those long red fingernails on her? Terrifying doesn't even come close to describing them."

An actual shudder ran through me as I thought of how Diane liked to prick those fingernails into people's chests.

"Addy, you've got to set boundaries with her. If you don't, she'll act like she's running the place. Trust me, I speak from experience. When she joined the bookstore's book club last month, she tried to take over. She even wanted to discuss the fact that I served chocolate cake instead of apple cake. But I made it clear that it's my store and my book club. That means I get to choose which cake is being served – apple, chocolate, or whatever kind of fruit that can go into a dessert."

I sighed. "I just don't know if something as trivial as

which kind of cake will get served is something worth fighting over with her."

"It might start with cake, but if you don't stop her, it'll end with Diane wanting her name on the lease or something. Besides, I didn't have a fight with her. I'm not *that* brave. It's still Diane we're talking about. I handled it in a more subtle way."

I laughed. "Subtle? You asked Alex to talk to her."

"Yeah, you're right. We're both chicken shits."

I rolled my shoulders back and forth to relieve some of the tension that had been building up in them. Between Diane's demands and Justin's silly comments, I'd had enough for one day. "What do you say? Shall we get out of here and grab a drink?"

"For sure," Suzie said. "Let me go talk to Alex for a sec and I'll meet you out front."

I put my coat on and strolled outside. Justin was standing near the wall next to the stairs, his hands in his pockets. We hadn't made eye contact yet, which meant I could duck back inside without him seeing me, if I was quick.

"Couldn't miss me for more than a few minutes, could you?" he asked, still looking out at the street.

How did he even know it was me?

I rolled my eyes in a futile attempt to let him know how annoyed I was. "You have eyes on the side of your body now?"

He turned his head in my direction and grinned. "Maybe. So, when are we meeting up to discuss our tasks for the Spring Picnic?"

"I can't right now. I have plans."

He cocked an eyebrow. His face twisted into a smirk waiting to break free. "Who said anything about right now? How about tomorrow?"

I threw my hands in the air. There was no escaping Justin, that much was clear. "Sure. The faster we get this over with, the better. Meet me at my house in the morning. Nine o'clock sharp."

"Yes, ma'am," he said, with a Southern accent he most likely learned from one of those fancy dialect coaches. Then he saluted me like I was a military sergeant.

I wanted to throw him a death stare, but for some inexplicable reason, a laugh came bubbling to the surface instead.

Justin pushed away from the wall, inching closer. "That smile right there is exactly what I've been waiting for."

He now stood close enough for me to notice the subtle scent of his laundry detergent. *Or for me to kiss him.* I let out a puff of air. Where did that thought come from? As if I'd ever kiss him.

"Me laughing at your impressions doesn't mean I like you now," I said before he could get any ideas into that annoyingly stunning head of his.

"I'll get you there," he said before walking down the stairs.

"Don't be late tomorrow. I only have one hour to talk to you," I called after him.

He turned around, the dimples in his cheeks deepening. "Give me some credit, Addy. I know you don't want to, but

I promise you it'll be worth it."

CHAPTER FOUR

"You're early," I said as I swung the front door open.

Justin looked at me with a surprised look on his face. I couldn't blame him, though. He had probably tried his very best to be on time and there I was, acting all catty. But it was true. He had showed up early and I was still wearing my faded Mickey Mouse pajamas. Plus, strands of my hair were sticking out of my messy bun. It wasn't exactly the image I wanted to convey. I should've gone home sooner the night before, but Suzie and I were having so much fun that I didn't want to leave.

"I am. Better early than late, right? Are you going to let me in, or should I wait outside for half an hour?" he asked, amusement written all over his face.

I opened the door further so he could step inside. "Come in."

He squeezed past me. "Nice outfit," he said, giving me the once-over.

"That's what you get for being early. I haven't showered yet."

"Go ahead," he said. "I'll wait."

I assessed the state of my living room. Was I really going to leave him alone in here? Not that there was anything suspicious lying around, but it was Justin. He would probably be able to magically make a pair of panties or something equally embarrassing appear from beneath my sofa cushions.

"Don't give me that look," he said with a smile.

"What look?"

He motioned toward my face. "The one that says you don't trust me."

"Well, can I? Trust you?"

He scoffed with fake disbelief. "Duh. Do you mind if I pour myself some coffee while you're in the shower?"

"Sure, go ahead. You'll have to make a fresh pot first, though. I haven't been up that long. And before you comment on that, I'm not lazy or anything. This is my free morning and I deserve to sleep in."

"Wow, relax, Addy. I wasn't going to say anything about your sleeping habits."

I gave him a curt nod. "Good. Now, make sure you behave yourself."

He laughed, then opened his mouth to speak, but I

stopped him short.

"Don't say it. Whatever dirty or childish phrase you were about to utter, don't."

I left him alone and headed for the bathroom. One look in the mirror confirmed my suspicions. I looked more like a junkie in serious need of a haircut than an attractive woman. I wondered if Suzie looked this tired as well after our girls' night out. Then again, why would I care what I looked like in the comfort of my home? It wasn't like I wanted Justin to like me. Or did I?

After showering and picking out some proper clothes, I headed to the kitchen in a hurry. I hoped Justin hadn't made a mess of things.

Luckily, he hadn't. I spotted a fresh pot of coffee, and Justin was busy wiping down the countertop. So he did have manners. Too bad he hardly showed them.

"Here, I've made you one too," he said when he saw me standing in the doorway.

I walked into the kitchen, and Justin slid a steaming cup of coffee toward me.

I put my hands around the cup and smiled. "Thanks."

He leaned on the small kitchen island with his elbows. "So, this is where you live, huh?" He let his gaze wander around the room. "It's nothing like I imagined it would be, and then again it totally is."

"Thanks," I said with some hesitation. I couldn't determine whether he'd given me a compliment or served me an insult.

I sipped on my coffee to avoid conversation. Wow. The

dark liquid tasted like he'd scooped it from the gutter.

"I guess you're used to assistants bringing you coffee?" I asked, shoving the cup away from me.

"Why? You don't like my coffee? I even used bottled water to make it," he said, pointing to a water bottle on the counter.

My face twisted. "No wonder the taste is off. That's rainwater from an old container filled with dirt and leaves."

"What? Why would you keep a bottle of rainwater on your counter?" Justin said, spitting out his coffee.

I lifted a shoulder. "For my plants, obviously. They prefer rainwater over tap or bottled water."

"Right, because that's totally normal. Ugh, I can't get the taste out of my mouth now." He scrunched up his nose and let his tongue run over his lips a couple of times.

I put my hand over my mouth and chuckled. "I'm sorry, but this is laughable. The fact that you can't even spot the color difference between rainwater and tap water makes me wonder just how much of a privileged life you're living."

He snapped his eyes to me. "You think you've got me all figured out, don't you?"

I shrugged. "Isn't that how movie stars live? Letting others do the dirty work for them?"

Now it was Justin who started laughing. "Wow. I've never heard so much prejudice and judgment coming out of your mouth."

"Maybe I should've worded it differently," I said.

I really should've. It wasn't fair of me to assume I knew

everything about him. Especially not since my ideas about his life as an actor were nothing but regurgitated clichés.

"I do have a butler who brings me breakfast in bed every morning."

My eyes grew wide with surprise. "You do?"

"Of course not, I'm just playing with you. You sure are gullible."

I wanted to scold him, but there were those dimples again. So instead of telling him off, I filled the coffee maker with fresh tap water and started brewing a new pot.

"Enough talking about my privileged life," Justin said. "You told me you only had one hour. Let's make it count."

"Uh-huh."

I couldn't manage to string a sentence together anymore. I was suddenly all too aware of the fact that I had a famous movie star sitting at my kitchen counter. And not just any movie star. No. Justin Miller. The guy I had hated for years, yet had this magic ability to confuse me. He put thoughts in my head I didn't want to have. Thoughts of him touching me. Of him—

"Addy?"

I blinked. "Yes?"

"You didn't hear a word I was saying, did you?"

"I'm sorry, I was thinking about… something else."

I grabbed two clean mugs from the cupboard and filled them both with coffee. Then I got a Tupperware container out of the cupboard, put a couple of homemade cookies on a plate and shoved it in Justin's direction.

"There. Now we can talk properly."

Justin picked up a cookie. "We need to decide on a theme first. And what movie we want to show."

"Milly sent me a list of approved movies. Let me grab it."

Justin chuckled. "Approved movies? Approved by whom?"

I scrolled through my phone until I got to Milly's email. I opened the document she had attached and showed it to Justin.

"I don't know, but I'm pretty sure no movie of yours will be on that list."

"And there she goes again," Justin said while going through the movies on the list.

"Don't take it personally," I said. "If your movies are as inappropriate as *In Dire Need*, then they will be way too, you know, for this town."

Justin put my phone down and folded his hands. "I *don't* know. Please enlighten me."

"I can't. I haven't seen any of your movies, but there's this scene I remember from *In Dire Need*… In the back of that bakery… You know the one."

He put his hand on his chin, pretending to think hard and deep. "What scene might that be? I seem to have forgotten."

My face turned beetroot. He was doing this on purpose so I would be forced to spell it out to him.

"Where the characters, you know. Do it," I whispered.

Justin's mouth twitched into a smile. Then he broke out into laughter, making his chair wobble from the sheer force of it.

"Why are you even whispering? Who do you think will hear us?" he asked, wiping tears of laughter from his eyes.

"Oh, stop it, Justin. You can be such a baby sometimes."

Maybe I should not-so-accidentally spill my coffee on his shirt as payback.

He turned my phone toward him so he could look at the screen better. "To be honest, this list sucks. There's nothing decent on here worth watching. All the movies are from before either of us were born. Can't we make some suggestions for more modern movies?"

"You can try. But Diane's on the committee. You'll never get her approval."

"Why not?"

I laughed. "Because she hates you. I'm sorry to break it to you, but you don't have a good reputation, Justin. Diane thinks you being here will jeopardize Asher's wedding. She even asked me to keep an eye on you."

Justin stared at me. "She did? What did you say?"

"That you're not my responsibility. It's bad enough that we have to work together for the Spring Picnic."

"Bad enough?" He laughed. "You secretly like me. Just admit it."

I snatched the last cookie right before he could. "In your dreams, Justin Miller."

A look boding trouble crossed his face. "There is a way to get Diane off your back, you know. Something that will ensure her that I won't cause any trouble, because you'll be right there to keep me on the right path."

"Stop talking in riddles, please."

He crossed his arms over his chest and looked at me with a mischievous grin. "You can be my plus one to the wedding."

I laughed so hard I almost choked on my cookie. "Your plus one? Over my dead body."

"Come on, Addy. It'll be fun," he cooed.

"Fun? I think our ideas of fun differ vastly."

Justin bit his lip. "If you agree and I turn out to be the jerk you think I am, then I promise I'll leave you alone forever. But I want nothing more than to prove you wrong."

"Tempting," I said. "But no."

"Addy. You know you want to. What can I do to make you say yes?"

I thought about his question for a moment. Would it be insane to agree? Probably. I was having enough trouble getting his pretty face out of my thoughts as it was. And I didn't want to start liking him. Then again, agreeing would also mean that I could ask anything of him, which could turn out to be a lot of fun after all.

I extended my hand. "I'll say yes. But only if you apologize for what you did to me back in high school. Publicly."

His eyebrows shot up. Ha! He wasn't expecting that, now was he.

After what seemed like an eternity of silence, he nodded and shook my hand. "We're on, Addy."

CHAPTER FIVE

It had been three days since I'd talked to Justin or even caught a glimpse of him. It bothered me, and I didn't want it to bother me. I was supposed to dislike him fiercely, not linger at the reception desk in the hopes of catching a glimpse of him.

Another thing that irritated me was not knowing what he was up to. Like, where did he hang out all day? In his room? At his parents' place? And where did he eat? I couldn't even ask Carter or Alex if they'd seen him. That would only raise questions I didn't want to be asked. His social media didn't give me any clues about his whereabouts either, as he hadn't posted anything in over a week.

The only thing I could do to get a dose of Justin was shut the curtains after work and watch *In Dire Need.*

When the credits of the last episode rolled over the screen, I grunted and threw the remote across the couch. I was supposed to hate him, not have all the feels after watching him on TV.

Justin was good at acting. Way too good for my liking. A part of me had hoped he would turn out to be a bad actor, but after two seasons of *In Dire Need*, there was no denying he was fantastic at his job. Not to mention the abs on that guy. Jeez, Louise, when his shirt came off in the season two finale I screamed into a pillow. Note to self, he could never ever find out he'd made me scream like that.

I pulled my knees up to my chin, wondering about the kind of person he'd become. To me, he was still Justin Miller, the jerk who had once tripped me in the cafeteria. My milk carton had exploded, sending white liquid in all directions. He and his friends had burst out laughing, telling everyone how much of a klutz Fat Addy was.

To make things worse, he'd crashed into me a couple of weeks later when he and his friends were practicing baseball throwing techniques in the parking lot. He ruined the science project I had to present in class that day. The entire school had seen me cry.

How could I forget something like that? Abs or no abs, acting talent or not… he had ruined my self-esteem. It had taken me years to come to terms with how I looked. I had lost a lot of weight two years ago and had learned to love myself, chubby hips and everything. But the memory of that nickname still lingered in the back of my head whenever I ate an entire box of cookies or gorged down a hamburger meal, something I should be able to do without feeling guilty. It was my body and my life, and I was the only person who had a say in either.

A beep indicated I had a new text message. I reached for my phone, thinking it was probably Suzie, but the text preview clued me in on the fact that it was some kid who had used a wrong number.

Unknown number: Do you have time to work on our assignment tomorrow?

I swiped the message app open to type a reply.

Me: I'm sorry, I think you've got the wrong number. The time for assignments is long gone for me. I left high school years ago.

Unknown number: Addy, it's me.

Me: How do you know my name? And how did you get this number?

Unknown number: Carter gave it to me. You'd already left. How many other men are you working on the Spring Picnic with?

Me: Is this you, Justin?

Justin: Bingo.

Me: I don't know if I have time tomorrow. I'll let you know something later.

Justin: Great. The picnic is in two weeks, so we can't keep postponing the work. Sleep tight.

I clenched my jaw. There was no way I was answering that text, wishing him a great night's sleep as well. He was acting all responsible and sweet right now, but it was probably just a matter of time before the other shoe dropped.

Or had he truly changed, like he had told me? I shook my head. There was no use speculating. The only way of knowing was to spend time with him, whether I wanted to or not.

***

I woke up early the next day and decided to get a head start on work. By ten o'clock I'd handled everything that needed handling. New guests would trickle in after lunch, as our check-in time started at two p.m. That gave me a few of hours without any urgent tasks. I fired off a quick text to Justin.

Me: I'm ready for our meeting now. I have four hours.

Justin: Wow, you don't give a guy much notice, do you? But okay, now works. I'm getting a head start. Meet you at

Jeff's barn?

Me: Okay.

I slid my phone into my purse and joined Carter at the reception desk.

"I'm going to be out for a bit to work on the Spring Picnic preparations. I'll be back by two, but if you run into a problem, don't hesitate to call me."

"A problem, like Diane?"

I giggled. "Shh. What if she walks in here and hears you?"

He leaned in closer and leveled me with a stare. "It wouldn't hurt her to hear the truth, you know. Don't let her walk all over you."

"Carter," I said, offering him a firm look.

He held his hands up. "Yeah, yeah, I know. I should always remain professional. Don't worry. If she drops by, I'll give her the royal treatment."

"Thanks, Carter. I'm going to check up on Duckota first. See you later."

He waved at me before returning his attention to the administrative work he was doing.

After making sure Duckota was safe and sound in her locked patch of garden, I went on my way. The barn was a pleasant fifteen-minute walk and it felt good to be out in the spring air. I spent way too much time inside and not nearly enough time in Old Pine Cove's stunning surroundings.

Colorful spring flowers bloomed in every patch of grass I came across. The mountains made for a picture-perfect backdrop, and with every step I took, I felt my anxious feelings about work and Justin seep out of me.

When I rounded the corner to Jeff's barn, I could spot Justin in the workshop that was attached to the barn. The doors were open and loud rock music blasted through a portable speaker.

Justin was wearing safety goggles and had stripped down to his jeans. His sweaty upper body glinted in the sunlight as he sawed wood, the muscles rolling with every one of his movements. I quickly averted my gaze before he could catch me drooling.

I stepped closer, coughing loud so as not to startle him. I didn't want to be responsible for him cutting into his hands.

He looked up, a smile spreading over his face, and put down his jigsaw. Then he cleaned the sawdust from his hands and stepped away from the workbench.

"What do you think?" he asked.

I looked around his work area. All I saw were cut pieces of wood and lots of sawdust.

"Um. Good, I guess?" I said carefully.

Justin threw his head back and laughed. "I know it doesn't look like anything yet, but I promise you I'm going to turn these pieces of wood into something amazing."

I laughed under my breath. "I don't know if your confidence is cool or annoying."

"There's nothing wrong with being proud of what you

do, Addy."

I picked up a triangle-shaped slat. "What is this supposed to be?"

He took the piece of wood from my hand, briefly touching my skin. His touch sent shivers all over me. Man, I hated my body for liking him.

"Were you even paying attention the other day?" he asked. "I thought we'd decided to build our own food stands. One for popcorn, one for cake and cookies, and one for pizza. This is going to be a pizza sign."

He held the sign next to his head, pretending to gobble it.

I nodded. "Oh, right. I didn't realize it was going to look this professional."

"Of course. I wasn't planning to just slap two planks together and be done with it."

"Why do you need me here if you're such a professional? I don't know the first thing about working with wood." I tried not to sound like a horrible person, but Justin had a way of eliciting snide remarks from me, like a magician who kept pulling rabbits out of a hat.

He cocked an eyebrow and grinned. I slapped him on the arm before he could say anything. It was so typical of him to want to turn everything I said into something dirty.

"Shut it. You know what I mean. Carpentry. Building wooden food stands."

He kept grinning, and his eyes watered up from a suppressed laugh. "So what if you don't know the first thing about wood? I can teach you."

I rolled my eyes. "I'm sure this kind of subtext works wonders for you in Hollywood, but this is Old Pine Cove, Justin. Your antics won't fly here."

He crossed his arms. "I mean it. In a non-sexual way. I know you're doing the decorations and baking the cakes, but there's no reason why we can't work on building the actual stands together. You could stain the wood. It would save us a ton of time."

"So basically, you want me to do your dirty work?"

His gaze pinning me in place. "You know what I don't get, Addy? You are such a sweetheart to everyone. In fact, I heard Leanne from Dave's Diner call you an angel yesterday. Your giggles and sweet comments seem to penetrate every part of this town. But whenever you're around me, you seem to turn into a little devil. All you have to offer me are snarky remarks. How much longer are you going to resent me for my past mistakes?"

I opened my mouth to bite back but changed my mind. Bickering with Justin was exhausting. Was that really what I wanted? To be even more exhausted than I already was? Maybe it would be better to try a different approach.

I bit my lip. "I'll try to be more angel-like in front of you. But don't test your luck. Consider yourself on parole."

"See? That wasn't so hard, now was it?" he asked with a smile.

I averted my gaze from his. Looking into his eyes for too long made me feel like I didn't know what to do with myself.

"Where's the stuff to stain the wood?" I asked.

He walked over to a box filled with paint brushes and cans. Then he put a cut piece of wood on two trestles before opening one of the cans with his screwdriver.

I put my hand in front of my nose. "That's a pretty strong scent."

"I know. Try putting on a dust mask. It might help with toning it down a bit."

He handed me a white dust mask and I turned it around in my palm. It looked anything but sexy. Not that sexy was necessarily the look I was going for, but still. Ridiculous wasn't a winner either.

"I'll manage, but thanks," I said with a smile.

Unless there was a sandstorm, there was no way I was covering my face with that thing.

I dipped one of the paintbrushes in the can and applied the stain to the wood with thick strokes. Justin returned to his workbench. He started measuring pieces of wood, drawing lines and circles on them with a pencil. We worked in silence for a while. Birds were twittering nearby, and a soft breeze ruffled the fresh tree leaves. I let out a contented sigh.

"This is a great work spot, right?" Justin asked. "Quiet, secluded, and beautiful."

I nodded. "It is. How come Jeff let you use his shed?"

"Our parents are old friends. And you know what it's like in Old Pine Cove. If someone needs something for a town event, nothing is too much trouble."

I smiled. "That's true. Don't you miss living here?"

He lifted a shoulder. "Sometimes. Old Pine Cove is still

home to me. Things hardly change around here. It's good to have a place that feels so familiar."

He lifted a fresh piece of wood onto his workbench and my gaze zoomed in on his bicep. I'd never seen one that big. Especially not one that seemed to be made from stone. I stifled a giggle.

"Are you checking me out again?" Justin asked. He didn't even look up from his work, but the laughter in his voice revealed he had caught me looking.

I shook my head fiercely. "I am not checking you out. I was concerned you might get a sunburn without your shirt on."

"Huh. Let me guess. You want to put sunscreen on my back?"

I held my paintbrush in the air, the wood stain dripping off the ends. "I'm already putting this smelly liquid on your wood. I think I'm good."

He looked at me with surprise. His mouth twitched, and he burst into laughter.

"You're something, Addy," he said in between heaves of laughter.

I couldn't help but break into a fit of giggles myself while I felt my cheeks getting redder with every passing second.

For the next hour, we worked in silence, him cutting wood, me staining it.

Surprisingly, the silence wasn't an awkward one. It was the kind of silence that felt comfortable and good. Like two friends watching the sunset together, each caught up in their own thoughts, the other's presence a blissful reminder that no one is ever truly alone.

Justin was the first to break the silence between us. "I could use a soda right about now. Want one as well?"

I nodded. "That would be nice."

He opened the lid to a cooler sitting in the shade, and looked inside. "Any preferences?"

"Do you have Pepsi?"

The ice clanked together as he rummaged through the contents. Then he closed the cooler and plopped himself down next to me, handing me an ice-cold can. "A Pepsi-loving girl is my kind of girl."

His kind of girl? Ugh, please. What a corny line.

He cracked his soda can open and held it in the air, waiting for me to do the same.

"To not having argued in well over an hour," he said.

Our cans crashed into each other, the dark liquid almost spilling over the sides.

"That doesn't count," I said.

Justin sipped from his drink. "Why not?"

"Because we haven't talked in well over an hour. It's hard to argue when no words are being uttered."

His eyes bore into mine. "Whatever works, am I right?"

He threw me a playful smirk before taking a swig of Pepsi. And unlike last time, I didn't feel the need to slap that adorably annoying smirk off his face.

CHAPTER SIX

"The menu is all set," Lilian said, checking boxes on the list in front of her. "So are the napkin colors. I confirmed the chairs and tables with the rental company. Rachel from Blooming Fun will deliver the flowers, and their colors will match the napkins and tablecloths. I'd say we're ready to go."

As Asher and Layla's wedding planner, she had a lot on her plate. I honestly didn't know how she managed to do it all. Catering to everyone's wishes, dealing with vendors, coordinating deliveries, dealing with Diane… I admired her ability to not once lose her calm demeanor.

"Everything's set on our end as well," I confirmed.

Lilian put her notepad down and took a sip of coffee. "Perfect. Three more weeks. They're going to fly by."

"Definitely," I said with a smile.

Three more weeks until the wedding and until I would get Diane off my back. Three more weeks until Justin went back west again.

Lilian got up. She gathered her things, then extended her hand to me. "It was a pleasure working with you today, as always. If any problems come up, please let me know immediately."

"I most certainly will."

I saw her out the door, happy that I could continue with my own pile of work. When I agreed to host the wedding at the inn, I never thought it would turn out to be this stressful. Even though all we had to do was provide the food, rooms, and backyard, it felt like a lot more. Probably because Diane kept adding tasks to my already long to-do list.

"Anything interesting happen while I was in that meeting?" I asked as I joined Carter at the reception desk.

"The couple from room 1E wants to have a bottle of champagne delivered to their room tomorrow. And they asked if we could provide some whipped cream as well."

I crinkled my nose and tried not to let my imagination run free. "What did you tell them?"

"That we can't do it because of health regulations, but that the local supermarket should have a can if need be. I also told them our walls aren't one hundred percent soundproof."

I slapped my hand over my mouth and giggled. "You didn't?"

He grinned. "Oh, I did."

Out of the corner of my eye, I spotted Diane coming through the front door. I quickly looked around to see if Duckota was on the loose again but couldn't spot her, nor did I hear any quacking. Good.

"Hello, Addison. Do you have a minute? I need to talk to you about a business proposal."

"Sure, give me five minutes," I said.

Diane nodded. "Alright. I'll be waiting for you in the lounge area. Oh, and could you be a dear and have Alex make me a cup of coffee? One and a half tablespoons of milk, no sugar."

She spun around without waiting for my answer.

"Who asks for milk by the tablespoon?" Carter asked, eyes wide with disbelief.

I laughed. "Beats me. Would she really notice if it were two full tablespoons instead of one and a half?"

"I'll call the kitchen and ask Alex to enlighten us," Carter said, picking up the phone.

I finished sending out two booking confirmations before joining Diane in the lobby. I didn't feel comfortable with her thinking it was okay to barge in here and demand I sit down with her as if I didn't have anything better to do. But telling her to schedule a meeting in advance like a normal person was something I didn't feel like doing either. I'd rather avoid being on the receiving end of Diane's criticism.

"What did you want to talk about?" I asked, seating myself in the chair opposite hers.

Diane put down her cup of coffee and folded her hands in her lap. "Addison, dear. Have you ever had any complaints about the cleanliness of your floors?"

"Not that I recall, no."

She put a finger over her mouth. "Hm. Well, this online review begs to differ."

She pulled a manila folder from her purse and handed me a piece of paper. "Why don't you read it out loud?"

"Out loud?"

She waved her hand at me, an irritated look in her eyes. "Yes, that's what I said. Go ahead."

I hesitated for a moment before I did as she asked, but figured I'd best get this over with. The sooner I could return to my daily tasks, the better.

"The Old Pine Cove Inn is a lovely place to spend a vacation. My husband and I went on a tour of the snow globe factory and loved exploring the hiking trails in the mountains. We always got a warm welcome after returning from our wonderful excursions. The place is impeccably clean. I only saw some breadcrumbs on the floor of the dining room once and they got cleaned up swiftly."

"Ha, see?" Diane said, a smug look on her face.

I frowned. "I'm afraid I'm not following, Diane. For starters, these people state how impeccably clean the inn is. And second, why do you have any interest in the cleanliness of my floors? Because I can tell you right now that there's no need to worry. The floors are clean and will stay clean for the wedding."

"Have you ever heard of the TurboVac5000 Diamond

Series?" she asked.

"Can't say that I have," I replied in all honesty.

"I thought not," she said. "You need one, Addison. And I can sell you one for a price that will blow your mind."

I shook my head in disbelief. Why would a retired person want to sell me a vacuum cleaner? Then it dawned on me that she had probably bought one herself and needed to get rid of it.

"You do know you can send most items back if you haven't used them yet, right? Why don't you contact the store where you bought yours?"

Diane let out a high-pitched laugh. "Oh dear, don't be silly. I'm not selling mine. I've got extra and I want everyone to experience the joy of cleaning with the TurboVac5000 Diamond Series. Your floors will have never looked this sparkly."

Okay, now it sounded like she was presenting an infomercial. Maybe she was rehearsing for a play? Nothing could surprise me when it concerned Diane.

"I appreciate the offer, but I don't need another vacuum cleaner."

"Yes, you do. And so do all of your friends," she said, her eyes full of desperation.

I leaned back in my chair. "All of my friends? Diane, what are you talking about? Please level with me."

She sighed. "I might have bought five hundred vacuum cleaners. But I promise you they are topnotch."

I gasped. "Five hundred? Why? How?"

Diane pursed her lips. "This charming man showed me

the power of these machines at the parking lot of the mall. He even cleaned my car for me, and I can confirm that my car's interior has indeed never been cleaner. The Turbo-Vac5000 Diamond Series does its job."

"Then why not buy just the one?"

She rolled her eyes and scoffed, as if I was a toddler who didn't understand a thing about the world. "Because that's not how it works. You can't just buy one. That would be a waste of money. You see, if you buy a hundred boxes from me, you can sell those at the inn. You'll make a huge profit. Can't you see what an amazing opportunity this is?"

I knitted my eyebrows together. "How much did you pay for all of those vacuum cleaners? Did you check that man's information? I'm thinking you might have been scammed, Diane."

"Scammed? By such a charming man?" Her eyes grew wide. I half expected them to shoot beams of fire at me. "Forget I said anything, Addison. Once I'm out of vacuum cleaners, you'll come begging for one. Mark my words."

She pushed the folder back in her purse and got up. I scrambled to my feet as well, and tried to rectify the situation. "It's nothing personal. I just want to help. Maybe you could get your money back somehow."

But Diane wouldn't hear it. She trotted toward the front door and I ran after her. She was unbelievably fast for an old lady, but then I almost crashed into her when she came to a sudden standstill.

A shocked look spread all over her face, and her mouth opened and closed like a fish. I followed her gaze up the stairs and looked right at Justin, who was dressed in nothing but a pair of denim shorts and black socks. A flutter of confusing feelings rushed through me, and I couldn't stop myself from staring at him.

Diane cleared her throat and shot me a death stare. "I'm starting to have second thoughts about hosting the wedding here, Addison. First, you don't seem to care about the cleanliness of your floors, and then you allow… this." She circled her hand in the air to where Justin was standing. "I thought this was a decent establishment."

Justin crossed his arms over his chest. "This *is* a decent establishment, Diane. There's no need to scold Addy. She's not responsible for her guests' actions, you know."

Diane's nostrils flared. "Mind your own business, Justin. And put some clothes on."

"Or what?" he asked.

I held my breath. How on earth did he find the courage to talk to Diane like that? He hadn't even blinked once during the entire ordeal.

"You listen to me very carefully, young man," Diane said, her red fingernail pointed at him. "I don't tolerate that kind of rudeness. Don't you dare ever talk to me like that again."

The vein on Diane's forehead throbbed so hard I was afraid it was going to burst. She stomped away and slammed the front door shut, leaving the two of us speechless.

"What was that all about?" Carter asked, joining Justin and me in the lobby.

"I think Diane has gotten herself into some kind of

pyramid scheme," I said. "She tried to sell me a vacuum cleaner. Apparently, she's got five hundred of them lying around."

Justin laughed, but quickly stopped when I shot him an evil look. "This is not funny, Miller. What if she takes the wedding elsewhere?"

Carter put a hand on my arm. "She's not going to do that. Where would she find a place to host a wedding on such short notice? Besides, her grandson wouldn't agree. Don't worry. Diane's just trying to get back at you for not buying one of her vacuum cleaners."

"You think?"

Carter nodded. "Absolutely."

"And you," I said, turning my attention to Justin again.

"What about me?"

"Was that really necessary? Why didn't you keep your mouth shut?"

Justin arched an eyebrow. "I don't let anyone tell me what to do. Especially not someone like Diane."

I put my hand on my hip. "I don't care. You can't jeopardize my business. And would it kill you to put on some clothes?"

"Why? You don't like my body?"

The way he wiggled his eyebrows while asking that question made me want to slap him. The arrogance of the guy was unbelievable. Every time I thought he wasn't as bad as I gave him credit for, he found a way to blow it.

I scoffed. "Get a life, Justin. Not everyone is interested in your looks."

I let my gaze wander to his naked chest for a moment, immediately regretting it. Seeing him like this made my body react in ways that were inappropriate to have about someone you hate.

"I'll put a shirt on if you go out with me tomorrow," he said.

My eyes grew wide. "You want to go on a date with me? Not in a million years."

"Who said anything about going on a date? I need to get out and have some fun, but not alone. Being alone is boring. Consider it a favor, not a date."

"This is the second favor you've asked of me, and they've both entailed me spending time with you. Don't you have any friends you could ask? Or, let me guess, they're all tired of you and you need new friends."

He casually shrugged his shoulders as if I hadn't just insulted him. "All of my friends live in L.A. Except for Asher, but he's too busy planning his wedding."

"Oh, I see. I'm the only person you can ask. Nice one."

Justin rolled his eyes. "It's not like that. I could ask anyone, but I want it to be you, okay?"

I bit my lip, trying to wrap my head around all of this. Why was Justin so set on going out with me when I obviously hated him? The guy sure loved torturing himself.

I let out a dramatic sigh. "Fine. I'll accompany you."

He smiled, showing off those damn dimples again. "Great. It's a—"

"Favor. It's a favor," I said before he could finish his sentence.

CHAPTER SEVEN

I was ready to go fifteen minutes before Justin was due to pick me up at my house. I'd spent an entire hour debating what to wear before settling on a pair of high-waisted jeans with a white tank top tucked in. I combined the outfit with my favorite pair of suede shoes and a long teal-colored cardigan. I wanted to look nice. Not for him, for me. And maybe also as revenge. If Justin saw how good I looked, he'd realize how wrong he had been calling me stupid names in high school.

I knew it was ridiculous to keep thinking about that. It was a long time ago and I should leave it where it belonged: in the past. Yet I felt the need to prove to him just how blind he'd been back then. For years, I'd been afraid to talk to guys, all because I felt I would never live up to their expectations of what a woman should look like.

No more. People would have to accept me for who I was, and what I looked like. I no longer cared if I fit their idea of the perfect woman or not.

I flopped down on the couch with my phone and scrolled through Instagram while waiting for Justin. The first picture to stare me in the face was one of him, a selfie he had taken while cutting wood at Jeff's barn the other day. It was captioned *One of my fav places in the world.* And in the background, there I was, staining wood with a look of concentration on my face.

Huh. Why hadn't he posted one without me in it? I didn't know what to make of that. The picture had half a million likes and thousands of comments. In a way, I felt weirdly proud for being in that picture with him, but it also made me frown. The least he could've done was ask me if I was okay with having my picture posted online. Then again, it didn't matter. I was nothing but a nameless small-town girl to the world. No one knew who I was, and no one cared.

A honking sound made me stop thinking about what all of this meant. I tucked my phone away and hurried outside to Justin's car, which turned out to be a sleek black Tesla. Figures. A more down-to-earth vehicle probably wasn't special enough for a star like him.

"Hey. Nice rental," I said as I got in.

He was silent for a beat while looking at me. "Nice outfit."

"Thanks. I wish I could say the same about you."

He shook his head, amusement written all over his face. "The cap and hoodie might be a bit too much, but the last thing I want is to be recognized. That's the whole point of this outing. I want to kick back and have fun, without whispering crowds of people around, trying to snap a picture of me eating a slice of pizza."

"It must feel like torture, being famous and successful," I said while clicking my seatbelt into place.

Justin picked up speed as we turned onto the main road, ready to leave Old Pine Cove. "I'm not kidding. I once had someone come up to me in a restaurant, asking if they could take my leftovers home with them. It's creepy. And I can never fully be myself. If I drink some beers, there will be pictures and rumors about me being an alcoholic. If I go to the movies with a friend who happens to be a girl, I suddenly have a girlfriend and a diamond ring in my pocket. I can never live up to people's expectations. I always have to be polite. Do you know what it's like to not have the luxury of having a bad day? I'll tell you, it's exhausting."

"Well, if you put it that way, it does sound like torture," I said.

"Told you so."

He turned the car onto the highway and I glanced over at him. Even though I'd made fun of his outfit, he looked incredibly sexy. His hair spilled out from under his cap, which was barely visible because of the hoodie he had put over it. It was like double protection. I let out a giggle.

He threw me a questioning look, but I didn't give him the satisfaction of admitting what I'd been thinking about.

"Where are you taking me?" I asked instead.

"Roger's. It's a place in the city I used to go to every week when Asher and I both still lived in Old Pine Cove. They serve the best burgers you've ever tasted. And they have themed nights. Should be fun."

"What if someone recognizes you there? It hardly sounds like a low-key place."

"I doubt anyone will. The lights will be dimmed, and I have this," he said, pointing to the cap and hoodie pulled over his head. "Besides, we're not in some big city. I doubt people here watch my show."

I shook my head. "Jeez, Justin. What, you think people here don't have TV or Netflix subscriptions? Just because this is a small community doesn't mean we're dumb."

He rolled his eyes. "I never said people here are dumb. Why do you always need to twist my words like that?"

"Okay, maybe you didn't say it. You implied it."

A grin traveled to the corners of his mouth. "I did not."

"Let's not play that game," I said. "So, burgers, themed nights and dimmed lighting, huh? I'm not sure it's going to be my scene."

"You'll love it, trust me."

He put a hand on my leg and gave it a small squeeze. I stiffened. All I could do was look down at his hand burning into my leg. I could feel his touch all the way to my toes. Then, just as suddenly as he had put his hand there, he pulled it away again.

Half an hour later, we arrived at Roger's. We asked for a table at the back in the hopes that no one would bother us in a dark corner like that.

"I still don't know why I'm here with you," I said as I slid into my seat. "We're not even friends."

Justin leaned back in his chair, a lopsided grin on his face. "I had a burger craving. And I hate to eat alone."

I put my menu down and folded my hands. "That's such a rude thing to say."

My gaze was met with a look of surprise from him. "Rude?"

"It's like I don't matter at all. I'm nothing but a convenience to you. Some prop you can use just so you don't have to look pathetic eating alone. And you know that I don't even like you. Why would you want to have a burger with someone who hates you?"

Justin let out a puff of air, his features softening. "You don't hate me."

"Who are you to say what I am feeling?"

He leaned forward, our hands inches from touching. "Addy, I'm sorry I made you feel like a prop. You're not, okay? I don't always pick the best ways of saying something, I know that." He took a deep breath, then continued. "To be honest, I thought it would do us both good to spend some time together. Maybe if you get to know me, you'll be able to see me in a different light. And for the record, I like hanging out with you. Despite the fact that you're convinced you hate me and serve me snarky comments all the time."

"You were the one who started that back in high school."

He held his hands out, palms up. "You're right, I did,

but I also apologized. If you can't look past what happened when we were younger, fine. But you can't expect me to keep groveling forever."

He picked up his menu, signaling the end of our conversation about the past. I slumped down in my seat and buried my head in my own menu. If I were completely honest with myself, I had to admit Justin did seem like a changed man. I wanted so bad to give him some credit, but at the same time, I was terrified of him hurting me again.

Placing the menu back on the table, I let my gaze wander to his face. It was a pleasure to look at. I just hoped what went on behind those gorgeous eyes of his was equally pleasant.

I slowly exhaled my breath. "Let's call it a truce. For tonight. Then we'll see."

He laughed and held out his hand. "I'll take tonight to start with. Shake on it, woman."

Smiling, I pumped his hand up and down with mine. The warmth in his eyes was almost as electrifying as his touch.

Then I pulled back, not wanting to give this moment more weight than it deserved, and nodded toward the menu. "Have you decided yet?"

"Burger with extra cheese, onion rings, large Coke and a large portion of fries."

"Wow, you're hungry," I said, signaling one of the waitresses to our table.

"I love to splurge occasionally. My agent has me on a strict diet, but she's not here. I figure I'm allowed the occasional treat."

"That sounds like a nightmare to me. I love to bake, and someone has to eat all of those cookies and cakes I make," I said. "Not that I do that every day. I try to be conscious about what I put in my mouth."

Justin's brow arched up and he bit his lip to keep from smiling.

I rolled my eyes at him, my cheeks flushed. "Don't make everything dirty."

"I don't know what you're talking about," he said. "I for one don't care what you put in your mouth."

A cough made us tear our eyes away from each other. "Have you guys decided what you want to eat?" a waitress asked.

I wondered how much she'd heard of our conversation. I hoped none of it, but feared the real answer was all of it.

I slid down a bit in my seat. "I'll have a burger and onion rings. And some water," I added.

"Water? Come on, Addy, live a little," Justin said.

"I thought you didn't care what I put in my mouth?" I said in hushed tones.

His eyes sparkled with amusement. "You're right, I don't. Water it is."

He smiled at the waitress and placed his order. Then he folded his hands, giving me that same look his *In Dire Need* character gave his girlfriend right before he told her he loved her. A flutter of tingly sensations went through me, even though I knew that look didn't mean anything. I was flattered nonetheless.

"What's tonight's theme?" I asked. "Didn't you say this place has themed nights?"

I needed to change the subject, to talk about something else. Anything that didn't involve him making me feel... special. Because I knew that was all my imagination's doing. The way he charmed everyone was nothing more than a habit he'd cultivated while living in Hollywood. It had to be.

He nodded at a door leading to a room in the back. "Everyone who buys a meal gets a free ride on the mechanical bull. The person who lasts the longest receives a voucher for a free meal. There's a winner every hour."

"Let me guess. You want us to try and win?"

His face lit up. "Oh, yeah, I do."

I let out a laugh. "I'm not going to stop you from climbing onto that bull, but I'd rather stand by and watch."

I thought he was going to push it further, nag me to join him on the bull, but all he did was shrug. "Sure. You don't know what you're missing, though. But I respect your decision."

Our food arrived and we both dug in. I hadn't realized just how hungry I was until I took a bite of my hamburger.

Justin motioned to my burger with his head. "So, what do you think?"

"You were right. Best burger ever," I said in between bites.

Another grin made his eyes sparkle. "I hate to say I told you so, but..."

I rolled my eyes at him, feigning irritation. His comments had started to feel familiar and safe instead of insulting or arrogant. I couldn't even remember why I'd made such a big deal of going out with him. This wasn't so bad. We were both enjoying ourselves and the burgers were delicious.

In the background, some indie rock blasted through the speakers, making me bob my head.

"Well? Is it working?" Justin asked.

"Is what working?"

He popped an onion ring in his mouth and chewed it before answering. "This. Are you having fun?"

"Yes, I'm enjoying myself."

It was true. I spent so much time holed up in the inn and my own little world that it felt good to go out and enjoy an outing like this.

"Good. You needed it," Justin said.

"What makes you say that?" I asked.

"You've done nothing but work your ass off these last couple of weeks. For Asher's wedding, your inn customers, the Spring Picnic… I figured you might want to forget about your responsibilities for one night. And judging by the smile on your face, I was right."

"Nothing beats helping the girl who loves helping others, does it?"

Justin put his hamburger down and folded his hands. "It's not as if I get a kick out of it. I think you might be working too hard. It's not healthy to push yourself like this. You were the same in high school. Always putting everyone's needs before yours. Studying hard to get straight A's and keep your GPA average above four point two."

I laughed. "How can you even pretend to know what my GPA was, let alone what I got up to after school? You hardly talked to me in high school, Justin. And when you did open your mouth to speak to me, nothing great came out."

He stared me down, that look in his eyes sending goosebumps all over my body. "That doesn't mean I didn't have my eye on you the whole time, Addy."

His words took me by surprise. I wanted to ask him if he was joking, but before I could speak, a group of giggling girls appeared at our table.

"Justin Miller? Oh my God, I can't believe it's really you. Will you sign something for me?" one of the girls asked.

She was about to flash her boobs to Justin, but her friend stopped her just in time. Good. This wasn't a brothel, and Justin was having dinner. I was positive they would come to their senses and leave us be any minute now.

"Can I take a picture?" another girl asked, shoving her phone in Justin's face without waiting for his reply.

"And can you sign something for me as well?"

Another girl pushed to the table, almost knocking my glass of water over. "Oh, will you follow me on Instagram?"

So maybe these girls didn't have manners at all. They certainly didn't look like they were planning on leaving us alone soon.

Justin threw me an apologetic look, then slipped into his role of Hollywood star to please his excited fans.

And just like that, the magical moment we had shared was gone.

CHAPTER EIGHT

"I'm so sorry about that," Justin said as he slammed the door of his car shut.

After those girls had approached him at our table, word had spread, and we had to flee Roger's after an hour of being constantly interrupted. I didn't even get the chance to watch Justin make a fool of himself on the mechanical bull, nor could I taste the strawberry cheesecake that was supposed to be 'exquisite' according to the waitress.

I didn't mind leaving, though. While Justin got showered with attention, I just sat there, watching the entire thing. No one cared that I was sitting at the same table. They only had eyes for him. Which, in a way, I had to admit was understandable. He was the famous actor, whereas I was an unknown small-town girl.

Kudos to Justin, though. He was a master of staying friendly and patient, signing autographs, posing for selfies… How it didn't drive him crazy, I had no clue.

I wedged my purse between my feet and clicked my seatbelt into place. "It almost felt like a zombie apocalypse in there, the way those girls came at you in a never-ending stream of swoons and screams."

"I didn't think people would recognize me around here," he said.

He looked genuinely confused, even though I couldn't figure out why. Surely, he must realize how famous he was?

"You might want to start the car," I said, nodding toward a new group of women. Their star-thirsty eyes scanned the parking lot, no doubt hoping to catch a glimpse of Justin and turn his car over or something.

He gripped the steering wheel tight and gunned it back to Old Pine Cove. But instead of dropping me off at the inn, he continued driving.

"Where are you taking me?" I asked.

"I know a place where no one will be able to find us. Unless they're Old Pine Cove townies, which those women certainly aren't."

"Um, okay," I said, shifting in my seat.

He eyed me and threw me an encouraging smile. "Don't worry, it's nothing creepy."

"Now I am truly worried," I said.

He laughed, keeping his eyes on the road. He took a left at the snow globe factory, heading for a place I'd heard of when I was in high school, but had never visited.

The narrow road snaked up the east side of the mountain, but the car had no problem keeping a steady grip. Pine trees lined the mountainside, standing tall and unmoving in the moonlight.

We were enveloped in a bubble of silence. The car was electric, so there were no roaring engine sounds, and Justin had stopped talking as well. It didn't feel awkward or weird to sit beside him in complete silence. It was almost as if the air between us grew more relaxed, yet more electrified the further up the mountain we went.

When Justin pulled into a clearing overlooking the town I called home, I swallowed. "You brought me to The Pine Lookout."

The spot was well-known amongst Old Pine Cove teens, as most of them had lost their virginity there. Not me, of course. No one had ever taken me up there before. I only knew the place existed because my friends used to talk about it.

"Relax, Addy. I'm not trying to get into your pants," Justin said, letting out a hearty laugh.

I crossed my arms in front of my chest. "First of all, you say it like you're repulsed by the idea of getting into my pants. And second… I wouldn't let you in even if you wanted to."

Justin turned off the engine and turned to me. "Woah, repulsed? I never said that."

"No, but your tone indicated it."

He pinched his brows together. "My tone indicated

nothing, Addy. All I wanted to accomplish was you feeling safe around me. I need to ask, do you hate all men, or just me?"

The sound of Justin's phone saved me from having to answer. He looked at the screen and let out an irritated sigh. "I'll be right back."

He slammed the car door shut and walked away. I couldn't hear what he was saying, but he didn't look amused. He kept shaking his head and gesticulating wildly.

I gazed around the car's interior, taking in the expensive leather seats with bespoke stitching and the control panel with the smooth design. I couldn't help but laugh. How did this happen? Me, sitting in an expensive car belonging to Justin Miller, the guy I couldn't stand.

Then again, was that still the truth? Things were shifting inside of me. Melting. As if every gesture and smile of his made the hateful feelings I harbored for him thaw. I even had to admit I wouldn't mind if he kept chipping away at the icy barrier I'd erected for him.

Another part of me was terrified to let him in, though. It would mean forgiving him for every past mistake, and I wasn't ready for that.

Justin got back in the car, slamming the door with a loud thud. "I want to apologize for leaving you to take that phone call, but I feel as if this entire night has been nothing but a string of apologies."

"No worries," I said. "Everything okay?"

I searched his face for answers, but he was good at hiding them. He was an actor after all. He locked his jaw and smiled. "It's all good, nothing to worry about," he said.

Yet I couldn't shake the feeling that he wasn't being entirely honest with me.

"How are you holding up with Diane breathing down your neck every day?" he asked, turning the conversation away from him.

I shrugged. "It's okay. She might have a tendency to drive people to nervous breakdowns, but Asher deserves a fantastic wedding day. Besides, Diane means well. She's stressed, that's all."

Justin shifted in his seat, angling his body toward me. "That might be true, but don't let her call all the shots. You're still the boss."

"I know, but I need the money. She's paying us a generous amount and I don't want to jeopardize that. Plus, I do like being a part of this wedding."

"Are you having money troubles?" he asked.

I shook my head. "No, no, it's nothing like that. I've…"

"You've what?"

I pulled my eyes away from his face and stared out the window. "Nothing, you'll think it's silly."

"I won't," he said, his voice soft. "You can tell me."

His honest-sounding words made me turn my head back in his direction, and I took a deep breath. "I've got my eye on the patch of land next to the inn. I'd like to buy it and turn it into a petting zoo, but the bank won't give me a loan unless I can pay at least twenty percent of the price upfront."

A big smile spread across Justin's face. "If this works

out, you have to buy an alpaca. They're such funny creatures."

"Do you have any idea how much alpacas cost? Some are being sold for ten thousand dollars," I said. "Each."

"Maybe you should consider jumping into Diane's pyramid scheme then. Didn't she say you could make a big profit off those vacuum cleaners? You know, the ones someone sold her at a parking lot? Because that's not shady at all, am I right?"

I laughed while shaking my head. "We shouldn't make fun of her like that."

"Why not? She's not afraid of being blunt with you. Come on, Addy, you don't have to be nice to everyone all the time. What do you want to say about Diane that might offend her?"

"I shouldn't."

He gave my shoulder a playful push. The sensation felt oddly fantastic. "She can't hear you. And I won't tell her. Just let it out."

I bit my lip. "Okay. Her perfume smells like she's been using the same bottle for the last thirty years," I said.

"There, that wasn't so bad, now was it?" Justin grinned at me, his smile thawing another icy layer.

I shook my head. "You bring out the worst in me, Justin Miller."

"Aw, you love that about me. I'm the only person you feel comfortable enough showing your inner bad girl to."

"Don't flatter yourself. People have seen my bad girl side before," I said, trying to sound cool.

He threw me a look that called me out on my bullshit. "Sure."

"Fine, you're right," I said. "Other people don't know that part of me. But the fact that you do, that I get snappy with you sometimes… That's because you're not the nicest guy. You can be so full of yourself sometimes."

"Who else would I be full of if not myself?" he asked. "There's nothing wrong with being confident, with speaking your truth and being proud of what you've achieved."

I cocked my eyebrow. "There's nothing wrong with modesty either."

He leaned back in his seat, shoving his hands in his pockets. "I guess we'll have to meet in the middle then. I'll tone my famous actor vibes down, and you speak up for yourself more often."

"It couldn't hurt to try," I said. "But I'm not convinced you can do it. It would mean you'd have to stop posting selfies on Instagram, looking all brawny and smug."

"I'll put a paper bag over my head next time. That'll help with the smug looks. The muscles… Yeah, can't do anything about that. If you have them, you might as well show them to the world," he said with a grin that set my insides on fire.

As I looked at him, a relaxed smile on his face, hands resting in his pockets, hair spilling out from under his cap… I caught a glimpse of the guy he was without the labels the world had given him. In the tiny confines of this car, he was no longer Justin Miller, award-winning actor with the dazzling smile and the overconfident talk. In here, he was Justin Miller, the small-town guy who needed someone he could talk to without being afraid of having his words twisted. Someone who didn't blindly adore him. Someone… like me.

He'd told me he wanted me to feel safe around him. But what if he was looking for that same safety from me?

He had closed his eyes, his broad chest rising up and down with every breath. "This silence feels so good. I can't remember the last time I was able to hear nothing."

"Then why did you break it with your chatter?" I asked, laughing. "You never shut up, do you?"

He opened his eyes. "Stop it. Admit that this is nice."

I did nothing of the sort, but I did smile like a moron. Because he was right. It was nice.

I stared at the lights below, illuminating Old Pine Cove. Life was so simple around here, yet somehow Justin coming back had complicated everything for me.

"Thank you for having a burger with me, Addy," he said.

"Too bad I couldn't finish it in peace, thanks to your fans."

"We'll have to do it again then," he said, his words nothing more than a whisper.

I grinned. "We'll see about that."

In the distance, two headlights crept up the road toward us. Justin and I exchanged a look.

"I think that's our cue to get out of here," I said.

"You're right. I don't know who's in that car and what kind of activities they've got planned, but let's not hang around to find out," Justin said. He started the car and pulled away from the clearing.

I got my phone out of my bag, pretending to read a message. Instead, I slid it on silent and opened the camera app. I angled the phone so that I had a perfect shot of Justin and snapped a pic. Okay, five pics. I wanted to remember this night before the clock struck twelve and I'd be back to hating him.

CHAPTER NINE

I didn't have a lot of time to think about my outing to Roger's and The Pine Lookout with Justin the next day, as we were officially opening our new flower-themed rooms to the public. All ten of them had been booked, and I couldn't have been happier. It was exhilarating to see the inn grow thanks to the hard work my team and I had put in the last couple of years.

Since it was a big deal for us to expand the inn, I'd hoped Dad would travel to Old Pine Cove for the occasion, but he claimed he couldn't leave Florida. He was the head judge of an orange-peeling tournament and forsaking his commitments didn't feel right to him. Even though I had frowned when he told me, I did understand. I too found it difficult to let people down, or not keep my promises.

At ten a.m. on the dot, Rachel from Blooming Fun parked her delivery van in front of the inn. I'd ordered fresh bouquets to put in the new rooms, each flower arrangement matching the room's name.

"Would you mind helping Rachel unload?" I asked Carter. "I want to go over my to-do list one last time and make sure I'm not missing anything important."

"On it, boss," he said, heading out the door and down the porch stairs to the parking lot.

Once all the flowers were in place and I'd done a last check-up, I was able to breathe freely again. I was just sprucing the pillows in the lobby one last time when I felt a presence behind me.

"Got a minute?"

I turned around.

"Well, well, if it isn't Kermit the Frog. Holding a duck," I said as I let my gaze travel from Justin's face to his arms.

He shot me a firm look. "That fence is getting fixed today, Addy, and before you resist, it's nonnegotiable."

"I don't get a say in it?" I asked, in a tone that sounded harsher than I intended. The stress of opening these new rooms was getting to me. "I appreciate it, but we have a grand opening today. Distractions are the last thing I need."

He held out Duckota as if she was an exhibit in a crime case. "If you don't get this duck a proper habitat, she'll keep escaping. Maybe even during the grand opening."

I let my shoulders drop. It wasn't fair of me to go against Justin like this. He was doing me a favor and I should be thankful. But did I really want him working in my backyard when I had a big event to focus on? He'd probably have sweat rolling down his abs by the time he was done, eliciting lustful looks from every woman in a ten-mile radius. I might have disliked him, but that didn't mean I disliked how pretty his strong jaw looked, or his hair that asked to be pulled on while—

"I'll interpret your silent stare as a yes then." Justin's words pulled me from my thoughts. I was pretty sure my eyes had glazed over.

It took me a moment to remember we were standing in the lobby of the inn with people scurrying past to put the finishing touches on the new rooms. Pulling on Justin's hair and getting all warm and fuzzy about it weren't the thoughts that should be crossing my mind at a moment like this.

"Uh-huh, yes, go ahead," I said. "And thanks."

I made a quick exit, blabbing something about having to check upstairs one last time even though I knew that the rooms didn't need any additional checks from me.

I closed the door to the Begonia Room behind me and slid into one of the desk chairs. What had come over me? Why did visions of Justin's abs and bedroom hair dance before my eyes? I was supposed to hate him for… for… for what exactly? Making fun of me all those years ago? Making me doubt myself? Ruining my science project? Or did I hate him because he was nothing like I remembered?

I shook my head and stood up again. If I allowed those thoughts to go any further, I'd be lost. I couldn't do that to myself, especially not on such an important day.

As I descended the stairs, I spotted Rachel at the front desk. She was arranging bright yellow sunflowers in a large vase, working fast and focused.

"That looks amazing," I said.

My words elicited a smile from her. "Thanks, Addy. I've got a box of plant food packets for you as well. Just add one packet to every vase in about five days and your flowers will last longer."

"Thank you. I appreciate your help. The flowers make the inn look so fresh and inviting. And they smell heavenly."

Rachel put the last flower in the vase, then took a step back to look at her creation. "There. All set. Make sure to call me if you need anything else."

I saw her out the door, then took a quick bathroom break. A handful of local journalists would arrive any minute. The first guests staying in our new rooms were expected soon as well. I hoped everyone would love the flower-themed rooms. It was a risk making the kind of investment I had, but I believed it would be more than worth it. A lot of families and older people preferred to stay in a small place like the inn instead of the big resort up the mountain. And if I did get a petting zoo, I'd need more capacity for guests as well.

The next hour went by so fast that I hardly had a chance to take a breath. Carter welcomed everyone at the entrance, leading them to the front desk where I checked them in, and Hugo from *Old Pine Cove Weekly* interviewed a couple of guests for his article on the grand opening. So far, everything was going as smoothly as it could. In fact, maybe a bit too smoothly. We were expecting twenty guests to arrive today, but even after everyone who had booked a flower-themed room was checked in, people kept trickling in. I was about to approach a group of seven women dawdling in the lobby and ask them if they had maybe booked the wrong date, when three vans stopped in front of the inn. Dozens of women piled out of them, almost toppling over each other.

They bolted toward the entrance with a pace that made me take a few steps back. When they frantically came running through the doors, I scurried over to the front desk. At least the counter meant there was a barrier between me and the excited women.

"Where is he?" one of them cried out.

Before I could ask who she was talking about, they all bolted out through the back door.

"What's happening?" Carter asked, looking as afraid as I felt.

Hugo put down his beverage and called out to us, "I'm going after them. This is going to make a great article."

Carter and I exchanged looks before running after Hugo. The women were huddled together at the back of the yard, right next to Duckota's living quarters. Suddenly, things became crystal clear. They weren't there for the grand opening, or even to admire my duck. These women had somehow caught wind of the fact that there was a celebrity staying at the inn.

I balled my hands into fists. There was no way in hell

I was okay with this. Today was about my inn, not Justin freaking Miller. He always did this. He always needed to steal people's thunder.

"This is pure gold," Hugo said, his face beaming while he took photographs.

At least one of us was elated about this situation. I narrowed my eyes and zoomed in on my target. Justin was not going to know what hit him.

Carter shot me a worried look and placed his hand on my arm. "Are you sure you want to do this?"

I scoffed. "Oh, I am. We've got a reception planned here in one hour. I'll be damned if I let Justin screw this up."

Carter dropped his hand. Poor guy. I'd probably scared him with my reaction, but I didn't care. This was not about him. In fact, it didn't concern anyone but me and Mr. Famous back there, smiling and signing women's body parts. To think I'd fantasized about his bedroom hair hours before. Ugh.

I marched over toward the group of fans and tried to push my way to the front.

"Hey, stop it, lady," one of them called out, pushing me aside. "Wait your turn like everyone else."

My eyes grew wide. The nerve! I contemplated pushing her back but thought better of it. Bodily harm was not my M.O. and I wasn't going to make it so now.

"Yeah, back off. Show some respect and get in line like the rest of us," a girl with braces told me. How did she even get here? Didn't she have school to go to, or parents?

"Respect?" I said with a hiss. "I'll tell you what respect is. It's getting out of my way. I own this place, damn it, and if I say you let me through, you will."

I couldn't remember the last time I'd been this angry, but I did know it felt horrible.

My words didn't seem to impress them, as all I got were cold stares. I put my hands on my hips. "Anyone who doesn't get out of my way will be removed from the premises. And I won't hesitate to call your parents," I said, staring at the girl with the braces.

Those words seem to do the trick. The crowd parted for me as if I was Moses on a mission.

"Oh, hey, Addy," Justin said, oblivious to the drama that had just unfolded.

"A word, please. Inside." I tried to sound as casual as possible, but failed tremendously.

Justin motioned toward the women around him. "I'm kind of in the middle of something. Can't it wait?"

Carter had also made it to the front of the frenzied crowd, and coughed. "Don't anger her, man."

"Or what?" Justin asked, a stupid smirk on his face.

Of course, this was all fun and games to him, as always.

"She'll have you removed from the premises," one of the women said with a roll of her eyes, eliciting laughs from the others.

"I doubt it'll come to that." Justin laughed and continued scribbling down his autograph on a woman's arm.

"I've had enough of this," I cried out.

I snatched one of the signed pictures out of some

woman's hands and held it up. I might have gone officially certified.

"I swear I'll rip this thing to pieces," I said, waving the picture in the air like a mad person. "Everyone needs to leave right now."

Justin held his hands up in surrender. "Ladies, I'll just be five minutes."

I threw him the coldest stare I could muster.

"Or could be ten," he quickly added, then followed me into the kitchen at a leisurely pace.

"What's wrong with you?" I asked as soon as the doors were closed behind us.

I couldn't believe he'd made me lose it out there. Normally, I was reserved and sweet, and yet Justin had managed to bring out the worst in me.

He cocked an eyebrow. "There's nothing wrong with me. My fans showed up and I posed for pictures, signed some photographs. What on earth could you have against that?"

"I don't need a bunch of silly fans crowding the place. There's a reception about to take place outside and it's invitation only. Somehow I doubt these women will stop showing up."

Justin sucked in some air. "They won't. Look, this is what being famous is like, okay? Do you think I like it when this happens? I was enjoying the fact that no one in Old Pine Cove cares that I'm famous. Everyone here knows me from before, so they leave me be. But I knew it was only a matter of time before people would find out I was staying here."

I frowned. "How would anyone find out? It's not like we broadcasted you staying here."

"I have no clue, but they always do. And when it happens, I have to suck it up. It's part of being in the public eye. And I have a lot to thank these fans for. Without them, I'd still be doing regional commercials. Anyway, I don't expect you to understand."

His words sucker-punched me straight in the gut. "Why? Because I'm a clueless small-town girl and you're some Hollywood hotshot?"

"That's not what I meant, jeez. Besides, them showing up and checking out the place could be good for business, no? Maybe some of them will want to stay here in the future. You can thank me later," he said with a shrug.

This was unbelievable. I didn't need Justin's so-called business help and I certainly didn't need his attitude.

I clenched my jaw. "Make sure they're all gone in half an hour. Or go somewhere else and take them with you, I don't care."

I turned on my heel and stormed out of the kitchen. Maybe I was overreacting, but I'd be damned if I was going to let Justin Miller ruin another one of my projects. I was so done with him.

CHAPTER TEN

I succeeded in avoiding Justin for the next five days. Whenever I spotted him coming down the stairs or pulling into the parking lot, I scurried away, attending to some not-so-urgent-but-I-don't-need-him-to-know-that business.

I was happy that the rest of the grand opening had gone down without any additional troubles, but I still couldn't believe Justin's attitude. *I don't expect you to understand.* Ugh. As if I was dumb and clueless about the world. I understood perfectly. The one thing I didn't understand was Justin himself. When would he come clean about why he had really returned to Old Pine Cove? Asher's wedding was the obvious reason, but I suspected there was more to it than that. If the festivities were Justin's sole reason for heading back home, he'd have arrived a couple of days prior to the wedding, not an entire month in advance.

Secretly stalking him on Instagram hadn't made me any wiser either. Checking out his social media posts every hour had to stop, though. He had wandered into my dreams more than once. Completely uninvited, of course, as always. But no matter how frantically I waved an imaginary "do not enter" sign around in my head, my subconscious skillfully kept ignoring me. I'd even printed out a picture of him and put a big red cross over his face with permanent marker. Didn't help one bit. I still couldn't get him out of my head.

I closed the door to my office and strolled over to the reception desk. I was almost finished for the day, which put me in a good mood. Even though I loved my job, I was in serious need of some R&R. The thought of lounging on my couch in sweatpants, with my favorite ice cream guys positioned in my lap – Glen and Barry, obviously, considering my love life was nonexistent and the real thing was a bit too expensive at the moment – and watching some brainless reality show filled me with joy.

"Everything okay here? Any urgent matters to take care of before I head home?" I asked Carter.

"Justin called about a malfunctioning television in his room. He told me he's gone out for the night, but there's no point in postponing the repair, right?" he said in a careful tone. He looked at me as if the mere mention of Justin's name would make me spontaneously combust.

"No need to call someone. I'll go check on it myself," I

said, a bit too eagerly.

Damn you, brain. We're trying to avoid the guy, not barge into his room and mess his television up even further.

Oh, who was I kidding? I was dying to go up there and inspect every nook and cranny of his sleeping quarters. It would be such an inappropriate thing to do, but the idea made my pulse race with excitement.

Carter's eyebrow shot up. "Oh, okay. I wanted to tell you I could call someone. I didn't realize you knew how to fix electrical appliances."

I waved my hand at him as if he'd said something silly and I had everything under control. "Well, you know. I picked up some knowledge here and there."

As long as Carter didn't ask me to fix anything for him as well, I'd be good. I sucked at anything remotely technical, even with a user manual right there next to me.

I walked up the stairs to Justin's room and knocked on the door. Good, no answer. The coast was clear.

I pushed the door open and tiptoed inside. The television was mounted to the wall at the opposite side of the bed. I glanced at it, then decided I wasn't going to touch the thing. I'd just tell Carter that the problem was so severe we'd have to call someone after all. It was better than risk getting electrocuted.

As I looked around the room, my ears worked overtime, trying to catch every sound. The last thing I wanted was Justin walking in on me.

I traipsed around the room, not even sure why, or what

I hoped to find in there. On his desk was a script for season three of *In Dire Need.* I reached to open it, but right before my fingers got ahold of the stack of papers, I let my arm go limp next to my body. This was wrong on so many levels. I shouldn't be snooping, no matter how curious I was. If Justin found me in his room, he could probably even sue me.

The basket with snacks that the inn provided to guests stood untouched on the desk. I rummaged through it and took a packet of peanuts out. It wasn't technically stealing if I replaced it first thing tomorrow, right?

I walked over to the bed and sat myself down on the edge. It was getting dark outside and I wondered what Justin was doing right now. Probably being chased by a fresh horde of women, and flashing his gorgeous smile in their direction.

I kicked off my shoes and carefully swung my legs onto the bed, tearing open the peanuts. After propping up one of the pillows, I let my head rest against it, taking stock of the room.

I knew the layout of the room by heart since I had decorated every single one of them. There was a snow globe on every nightstand, no matter the season. Old Pine Cove housed the oldest snow globe factory in the state after all. The bathroom door was positioned right next to the desk, and the closet had plenty of room for clothes and even skis.

I nibbled on a handful of nuts. So this was the view Justin had every night. The room where he did who knows what and studied his lines. The bed was so comfortable, I let myself sink deeper into it. It clearly had been an excellent idea to replace the inn's mattresses last year.

My eyes fluttered shut, but I forced them to stay open. I didn't want to risk getting caught sleeping in Justin's room.

Then again, Carter did say Justin had left for the night, and a fifteen-minute power nap was exactly what I needed.

No, no, no. I had to head downstairs, call someone to fix Justin's TV, and go home. I fisted the sheets, their softness making me sigh. Justin's scent was all over the bed. I took a deep breath.

Gah, none of this was helping me. I needed my brain to send a signal to my body to get up and get out, but the connection between the two was as malfunctioning as Justin's TV.

I didn't want to fall asleep, but I could let my eyes rest for a minute. Five minutes tops. I'd be out of there in no time.

***

I woke up in a puddle of my own drool staining the pillowcase. Classy. I yawned. How long had I been asleep? It couldn't have been long. Still, I had to get out of the room before Justin returned.

I sat upright and shrieked when my hand touched something hard. I flipped the light on. Right next to me on the bed I saw a person's shape. At least, I hoped it was a person and not some wild animal.

Dark hair peeked out from under the covers and a hand appeared at the top seams, pulling the sheets down. Justin greeted me with a lazy smile.

"What are you doing here?" I asked.

He ran a hand through his hair and laughed while propping himself up against his pillow. "I pay to sleep in this room, remember? The real question should be: what are *you* doing here? Do you sneak into other guests' rooms like this, or am I the only one?"

I glanced over at the television, still as dead as before. "I came to check on your television. It was nothing but routine business."

He looked at me with a gaze that told me he didn't buy my weak explanation. "Sure, routine business. Also, there's a peanut sticking to your forehead. Did you take those out of my snack basket?"

"No." Right on cue, the peanut fell onto the bed and landed next to the crumpled packet I'd devoured the night before.

Justin picked the peanut up and held it in the air like a piece of important evidence. "I would call this guilty as charged."

"I needed to see if the snacks we offer are of sufficient quality," I said. "We often conduct research like that."

The corners of his mouth twitched. I could tell he was having trouble not bursting out into a laugh. "That's quite the research. Sneaking into guests' rooms, then sampling their snacks before falling asleep in their bed."

I blinked. I had just slept in Justin's bed after eating his food. A lot of women would be jealous of me, but I didn't want him to think I was one of them, let alone be seen as unprofessional.

I jumped out of the bed like it was full of spiders. My eyes flitted toward the bathroom, and for a moment I contemplated escaping through the window, only to realize seconds later we were not on ground level and I might break my neck fleeing from this situation.

I cleared my throat. "It's the truth. I don't even like you, so why would I be here if not for the television?"

He laughed as if I had told him something utterly ludicrous. "You do like me, Addy. Why do you keep insisting you don't?"

Because you're irresistible and the only way I can deal with that fact is by telling myself I hate you.

"I'm sorry, I'd better go," I said, ignoring his question.

Justin smiled at me. "Fine, go. But one day I'll get the truth out of you. Do you need me to escort you to your house? It's three in the morning."

I gasped. "Three a.m.?"

What the heck? It was about eight when I came to his room and now it was the middle of the night?

"Why didn't you wake me up?" I asked.

He shrugged. "You looked so peaceful that it didn't feel right to do so. You were even smiling and sighing in your sleep. But I was exhausted and the thought of spending the night on the floor didn't appeal to me, so I slept next to you. I promise I stayed on my side the entire time."

I put my shoes back on. "Well, thank you for letting me

crash here, I guess? No need to escort me, by the way. This is Old Pine Cove. The crime rate is almost nonexistent, and my house is just next door."

"Are you sure?" he asked.

I nodded. "Uh-huh. Sure I am."

Gah, now I sounded like that green guy. What's his name? Yes, Yoda.

Justin put his arm behind his head and the covers slid down, flashing a piece of bare chest. "All right. Good night, Addy."

"Good night," I said, my cheeks burning with mortification.

As I carefully closed the door behind me and tiptoed downstairs, I kind of regretted him not pushing his offer any further. Maybe it would've been nice to have him walk me to my house after all. Then again, what if he had? It wasn't like I'd have invited him in for a drink at three in the morning.

I stepped inside my house two minutes later and headed straight for the bathroom to brush my teeth. After getting under my own duvet, I closed my eyes, but sleep didn't come. The exhaustion I had felt hours ago was now replaced by a feeling of loneliness tugging at my heart. My bed didn't carry Justin's smell, nor did it have those soft sheets I used at the inn.

I tossed and turned for half an hour before getting up again. I yanked a tub of ice cream out of the freezer and turned Netflix on, scrolling to my 'watch it again' list. As soon as I pressed play, the now familiar intro to *In Dire*

Need came on and I couldn't help but smile as Justin's face filled the screen.

CHAPTER ELEVEN

"What on earth is this truck doing here?"

It was the day before the Spring Picnic and a big delivery truck with "PMS" painted on the sides in bold letters was blocking the street right in front of Dave's Diner.

Dave himself was hauling a fold-up table to the town square, where several people were getting everything ready for the picnic and open-air movie theater. His face was bright red and he shook his fist in the air, cursing the truck and its contents.

The delivery driver looked at him wide-eyed, then shook his head and mumbled something about how every town had their own collection of wacko people.

"What's going on?" I asked, joining Dave on the sidewalk.

"None of my customers can get inside. And their view is blocked by this truck," he said.

He made it sound as if there was an entire cruise ship parked in front of his diner instead of a standard-sized Parcel Mail Services truck. Normally, I hated to encounter PMS, but this was a different type altogether. And the view Dave was talking about? It was just a regular old town square, not some jaw-dropping tropical beach or summit.

I approached the driver. Someone had to take it upon themselves to find out what was going on. "Are you delivering stuff for the Spring Picnic?" I asked in my friendliest voice.

"I honestly don't know," the guy said, shaking his head. "All I've got is an order form for five hundred vacuum cleaners with clear instructions to drop them off at the town square. That's all the information I can share, sorry."

I watched in horror as the guy kept stacking all five hundred boxes of vacuum cleaners on the grass. A small crowd of people gathered on the pavement around me.

Fifteen minutes later, news of the enormous delivery had spread, and Diane came rushing toward the town square.

Diane and Dave were on good terms with each other, but judging by Dave's glaring eyes, their comradery might be pushed to the background, at least for now.

"Good, they've arrived," Diane said.

She gave the boxes an approving look.

"Good?" Dave asked, seething. "These boxes take up

half the town square. It's like you've taken it upon yourself to build a replica of the Great Wall of China in our small town."

"There, there, Dave," Diane said, swiping some imaginary speck of dust off her cream-colored sweater. "No need to get angry with me. I can't help it that I've got such great business opportunities coming my way. Besides, the mayor has given me his explicit approval."

Dave scoffed. "Of course he has."

As the mayor's mother, it came as no surprise that Diane had gotten some privileges. But her acting like she *was* the mayor might have gone a bit too far. Old Pine Cove thrived on a sense of community. Angering Dave was not a good move, unless Diane wanted her next sandwich to contain something gross.

"Tell you what, to make things right, I'll give everyone who buys a TurboVac5000 Diamond Series a ten percent discount."

The crowd went silent, none of them wanting to break the news to Diane that these vacuum cleaners were not a top priority to them, especially not at the price she was selling them for.

"Discount or no discount, that doesn't solve the problem of this truck blocking the pavement," Dave said.

Diane shot him a closemouthed smile. "I'm sure all the boxes will be unloaded soon enough."

Dave put his hands on his hips to let Diane know that was not the solution he was waiting for.

All that was missing now was a lonesome tumbleweed

rolling by, and Dave and Diane drawing their guns. I wondered who'd win in a standoff like that. It would be a close call, for sure.

As I had stuff of my own to take care of, I decided it was no use staying on the sidewalk and watching a heated discussion unfold. I turned around and walked over to the spot where Justin and I were setting up our food stands.

"Do you really need to work on this shirtless?" I asked, motioning toward his bare chest. "This place is crawling with kids, you know."

Justin put down his drill and narrowed his eyes as he looked around. "Oh yeah, where are those kids you're talking about?"

I followed his gaze around the square. The swings at the far end were deserted, as well as the slide. Milly was placing colorful quilts on a table and Mr. Rogers was trying to get his electric wheelchair over an uneven patch of grass, his tires not getting any grip whatsoever. Luckily for him, a group of seniors sporting *Bingo Was My First Love* shirts came running to his rescue.

Fine. There were no kids in sight, but they could arrive any minute.

"Take this," Justin said, throwing something my way.

The object landed at my feet before I could even stretch my arms and try to catch it. I crouched down and picked it up.

"A packet of peanuts?"

He laughed. "Yeah, what else? You love nuts so much that you sleep with them."

"I don't love nuts *that* much," I said. "I actually prefer a different kind of nuts. Not human nuts, walnuts," I quickly added.

Gah, I had to stop with the nutty talk.

I shoved the gift in my pocket. "What do you want me to do?"

He handed me a big wooden model of a plate. "Hold this so I can attach it to the roof."

He held the other side and attached it, then came over to my side. I gripped the piece of wood like it was a matter of life and death. He was standing so close to me that I almost got pushed into his chest hair. I turned my face, but that didn't help matters either. Now my other cheek was pressed against his bare chest. I squeezed my eyes shut and tried to think of anything but him and how good his skin felt on mine. It was no use, as I was still inhaling his ridiculously awesome scent. Even his armpit smelled nice, all manly and intoxicating.

It wasn't fair that Justin had everything going for him. Good looks, a great job, lots of money, *and* a non-smelly armpit. No wonder he often came across as arrogant.

"You can let go now," he said, drilling the last screw into place.

I pulled my face away from his chest and let out a long breath.

He wiped some wood dust off his jeans and took a step back to admire his creation. "Not too shabby, right?"

I had to give it to him, the guy knew how to build something appealing from nothing but a couple of wooden planks.

He held his palm up for me. I high fived it. I was still feeling confused and flustered from being smashed into his body, though. Okay, I knew that it didn't mean anything. Not anything romantic anyway. There simply was no other way to attach the plates to the roof of the food stand without him standing close to me.

"Oh, look, it's Suzie," I said, spotting my friend passing the Great Wall of China and heading our way.

Any excuse to step away from Justin would do. I didn't know if he felt the tension between us as well, but to me, it was making the air so heavy that I was afraid I'd get crushed.

"This is looking good. Great job, Justin," Suzie said.

Her eyes twinkled when looking at him.

"Thanks," he said before walking over to the other side of the stand.

I slapped her on the arm and pulled her out of hearing-distance from Justin. "Stop doing that."

"Doing what?"

"Checking him out with that look," I whispered.

She let out a laugh. "Oh, come on. I love Alex fiercely, but this is Justin Miller. As in famous and gorgeous actor. Any woman would have a peek if they were standing so close to him. It doesn't mean anything. You on the other hand..."

"Me what?"

She leaned in closer. "I think you secretly adore the guy."

I scoffed. "I do not. Do I hate him less than I did last week? Sure. But there's a long stretch of feelings between hating someone and adoring them."

"I won't bring it up again. Not today anyway," she said. "Are you all set for the Spring Picnic tomorrow?"

I nodded. "I need to bake some more cookies, but everything else is going according to plan."

"Well, if you need any help, let me know. I've gotta run."

"But you just got here," I said.

"I know. I was actually on my way to Sip'nBean to grab some coffees. Pippa's at the store all by herself and must be wondering where I am. See you tomorrow, Addy. You too, Justin," she called out to him.

"See ya," he said and gave her a little wave.

He had climbed onto a chair to put the finishing touches on our food stand. His tool belt sat snugly around his waist and every time he stretched to reach the back of the stand, his abs flexed. This was too much. Why was he torturing me like this? I needed a cold drink. And if that didn't do the trick, I'd hop into a cold shower.

"I'm going for a walk," I said in a high-pitched voice. "Do you want me to pick up something to drink on my way back?"

He motioned toward a cooler placed on the grass. "Thanks, but I'm all set."

I hurried away from the magical effect his chiseled chest had on me. This was so not me. I had never been this physically attracted to someone before. And especially not someone I had beef with. My last boyfriend was sweet, and we got along great, but he never made my pulse race. Not like this, anyway.

I left the town square and crossed the street to Sip'nBean. An iced coffee might seep some sense into me.

"Hi, Addy," Olive said. She was the most upbeat barista I'd ever met. "What can I get you today?"

I smiled at her and got a couple of dollar bills out of my purse. "A caramel iced coffee, please."

"Coming right up. How are things at the inn?" she asked while prepping my drink.

"Really good, thank you."

"I heard you're thinking of opening a petting zoo. That's so exciting."

I grinned. "I know, right? It's going to be amazing."

Olive put my coffee on the counter, a dreamy look in her eyes. "I'd love to open a dog hotel one day. You'll give me some advice when the time comes, right?"

"Sure," I said with a laugh. Everyone in Old Pine Cove knew how crazy Olive was about dogs. She even ran a business on the side where she offered tarot readings for dogs.

I grabbed my drink and waved her goodbye before settling myself on the terrace outside. The May sun was giving her best effort. I loved days like these. Winter was nice too, as Old Pine Cove was the best place to spend those months, but there was nothing like the allure of clear spring nights and the days getting longer and longer as time passed.

Asher and Layla's wedding would take place only ten days from now. It meant that a busy period would come to an end for me, but it also meant Justin would be leaving soon. Not that I wanted him to stay, per se. I doubted he would want to stick around here longer than intended. His life in Hollywood was probably an exhilarating one with new adventures every day.

Sometimes I wondered if I would have stayed in Old Pine Cove myself if it hadn't been for the inn. When my dad left for Florida after gushing about golf carts and oranges, he kind of assumed I'd take over the inn. I did, because I loved working with people and making sure all their holiday needs were met. But I'd never traveled far outside of my hometown. It was ironic, really. I spent all this time catering to people who were taking a well-deserved vacation, yet I never went on one myself.

I got my phone out of my pocket, my fingers automatically heading for the Instagram app. Oops, now the app was open, and I couldn't stop myself from scrolling. I looked up pictures Justin had posted himself, pictures he was tagged in by others, and pictures of his friends. His life seemed alien to me. Here I was, surrounded by beautiful mountains and people I'd known all my life, while he led a completely different life out there, chilling in the shadow of palm trees, frolicking on the beach, and attending parties in the Hollywood Hills.

A tiny part of me was intrigued by a life lived outside of the Cove, but I knew it would always be a fantasy, at least for me. I had responsibilities here.

Plus, I still had dozens of cookies to bake for the Spring Picnic, which meant I didn't have time to sit around and think about things that would never happen. I had to get back to work.

I got up, my chair scraping across the concrete. The package of nuts Justin had given me earlier fell out of my shorts pocket. I picked it up and tucked it back in safely.

Justin might be leaving in a couple of weeks, but at least I still had his nuts.

CHAPTER TWELVE

The next day, I arrived at the town square early. The picnic wouldn't be starting for another hour, but I wanted to be the first one at our stand. We weren't technically expected to man the food stand, but Milly had asked me weeks ago and I couldn't let her down. Justin agreeing to help as well was a bit unusual, but I wasn't going to argue with him about it. After all, I'd arrive first, smile all day long, help everyone who needed help, and I'd sell the most popcorn. Excuse me, the *best* popcorn. Why? Because I was planning on adding an extra scoop of popcorn to every serving I made so that Justin seemed like the cheap one.

Mean girl wasn't my middle name, far from it, and I also didn't wish failure on Justin. But I did want to be the best when it came to the Spring Picnic. He already had his looks and fame working for him. And the dimples. He had all the advantage. I guess I didn't want him to steal my Spring Picnic thunder. This was the third consecutive year I'd made food for the event and I loved the way people gushed about my baking skills each year.

I placed ten containers on the table, each one filled to the brim with my signature homemade cookies. I wouldn't open them until right before the start of the event so they stayed as fresh as possible.

The pizza stand Justin had made looked amazing as well. As we couldn't man two stands, Helen had agreed to serve the pizza slices.

I pulled one of the folding chairs closer to the table and sat myself down. Since there was still an hour to kill, I used the time to read a book. With the upcoming wedding, Duckota escaping, and the Spring Picnic, I hadn't been able to sit down with a book in I didn't even know how long. At least Duckota hadn't escaped since Justin had put a bigger fence around her piece of the yard.

I let out a blissful sigh and opened my book. It was part of a feel-good series that took place on a cruise ship. As I'd never had the chance to take a cruise before, I lived vicariously through these characters.

Just when the main character was about to go water rafting with a handsome guy, a voice yanked me out of my blissful experience.

"Are those homemade cookies?"

Five minutes. Really? That's all I'd gotten? Five minutes

of peace? I put my book down and got up. Justin was eyeing my cookies and reached for one of the containers.

"Stop, no touching my cookies," I yelled.

His hand hovered mid-air. "Why not?"

"Because they're for paying customers," I said, shoving the containers away from his greedy hands.

"Okay, how much for one of those chocolate chip cookies?" he asked.

He'd already gotten his wallet out of his back pocket.

"For you? Ten dollars," I said with a grin.

I didn't mean it, of course. No one in their right mind would pay ten dollars for one cookie, but Justin handed me two fivers, grabbed one, and took a bite.

Then he started making sounds that could only be described as bedroom noises. "Hmmm, oh yes. Wow, Addy. This is something else. I've never had a cookie this delicious. Hmmm."

The sounds that left his perfectly formed mouth stirred my insides. I tried to cover my ears, but that only made me look like a lunatic.

"I'm going to need another one of those," he said, reaching for his wallet again.

Sweet mother of baby goats, there was no way I was letting him get off on one of those cookies again.

"Uh, there's a one cookie per person limit."

He slowly nodded. "I guess that's not a bad idea. Otherwise they'll be sold out after half an hour."

"That's exactly the reason why I came up with that rule."

It was a blatant lie, but he didn't have to know that. Although it might be a good idea after all. Every year, I had to swat people away from my cookies, wanting to get their hands on a dozen of them.

Justin motioned to the other containers. "What other flavors do you have?"

"Banana oatmeal, regular banana, gingersnap, raisin, peanut butter, vanilla, and macadamia nut."

He smirked. "Nuts, of course. How appropriate."

"I didn't use your nuts. The ones you gave me, I mean, not your real nuts," I said, gesturing at his crotch.

What was wrong with me? *Not your real nuts?*

Justin let out a bellowing laugh. He even had to place his hand on his perfect stomach to stop him from shaking too hard.

I rolled my eyes. "Yeah, very funny. Not immature at all."

This was just great. Now I was going to think of Justin's nether regions every time someone ordered a macadamia nut cookie.

"I love how you mess with me in the most innocent way," he said, shoulders still shaking with the aftershock of his laughter.

"Get a grip, wonder boy. People will start arriving soon and the popcorn machine needs to warm up."

I had no clue whether or not popcorn machines needed warming up, but I figured it couldn't hurt either way. At least it would get Justin to stop laughing and think about other things than cookies and nuts.

We went to work and greeted our first customer exactly

forty minutes later. The Spring Picnic had been an Old Pine Cove tradition as long as I could remember. People would fill their basket with all the treats on offer, then enjoy each other's company while a live band played in the background. The night always ended with a movie. The atmosphere was relaxed and friendly every year, and today was no different.

My cookies did sell way faster than the previous years, but I think it might've had something to do with my cookie colleague. The girls from the bingo club couldn't stop giggling and blushing when Justin handed them each a bag of popcorn and a cookie. They kept talking about how they'd known Justin as a baby and how he'd grown into such a handsome, eligible bachelor. Their words, not mine.

I served a lot of inn guests who told me they loved all the activities that Old Pine Cove had to offer during spring. I let every single one of them know about the other fun events that were held annually in Old Pine Cove, like the Winter Walk, the Snow Ball, and the Autumn Festival. Couldn't hurt to let them know and have them come back during a different season, right?

Plus, their positive feedback would do wonders for my Yelp score. Not that I needed it – I had been the proud owner of 4.5 Yelp stars for years.

Before the picnic, I'd been afraid that our peaceful day might get crashed by another group of Justin's fans, but I hadn't spotted any star-crazed women so far. Apart from the local ones, but they were harmless.

By the time the movie was about to start, all we had left

were about a dozen servings of popcorn.

"Your cookies sold well," Justin said. "Not surprisingly. They were delicious."

"Thanks, I'm glad you approve of them. You know, everyone's settling into their seats for the movie. I can man the stand on my own if you want to leave."

"Nonsense. I'm staying. Besides, we can watch the movie from here as well."

He plopped down in one of the folding chairs. He stretched his arms above his head and flexed his toes. "I can't believe how good it feels to finally sit down."

"I wish I could put my feet up," I said. "They're killing me. I'm used to walking around all the time, but today felt like a marathon."

Justin got up again and picked up a chair that had been abandoned near the gazebo.

"Here. Now we can both put our feet up," he said, plopping the chair in front of us.

He kicked his shoes off, swung his feet up, and let out another one of his toe-curling moans. "This feels so good."

Why did every sound he made seem so seductive?

I longingly looked at the chair Justin had put in front of us. It seemed a bit too small for two pairs of feet.

Justin cocked his eyebrow. "What? I don't have a contagious foot disease, you know. Just put your feet up and enjoy the movie."

I reluctantly slid my flats off and placed them beside my chair. The opening tunes to the movie blasted through the speakers. Justin's eyes were glued to the big screen, or at least he was pretending. I couldn't imagine him being this captivated by *Singin' in the Rain.*

That's right. The entire committee had vetoed every single one of our modern movie proposals. They said they were "too risqué", even though I didn't understand what could be considered racy about *A Dog's Tropical Vacation* or the latest *Wizard Kids* remake.

I put my feet on the edge of the chair Justin had placed in front of us and let out a contented sigh of my own. My feet started tingling, happy to finally get some rest. Just then, Milly stopped at our stand to get herself a bag of popcorn.

"I'll get this one," Justin said.

Once Milly was on her way, Justin sat back down, only this time, his feet touched mine. Just the tip of one of his toes, really, but the sensation set me ablaze. I couldn't possibly focus on Gene Kelly now that our extremities were touching, but still I fixed my gaze on the screen.

After half an hour, my neck started to hurt. It was really hard not to move it an inch, and I finally caved. The moment I stole a glance at Justin, he stole one at me. A lazy smile made his face look even better than usual.

He opened his mouth to speak, but I stopped him in his tracks. No doubt he was going to start giving me that nonsense about checking him out again.

"I'm flexing my neck muscles," I said.

I turned my head left, then right, in exaggerated motions. I didn't even stretch my muscles this far during Alex's yoga classes.

"Oh, yeah, me too," Justin said.

But instead of following my movements, he only turned his head to one side. Mine. He wouldn't stop staring at me.

"I need a bathroom break," I said in a high-pitched voice before fleeing the scene.

Justin got up as well. "Me too," he called after me.

I turned around, my hand on my hip. "You can't. What if someone needs popcorn?"

"They can wait."

"What if they can't?"

Justin caught up with me and laughed. "What if they can't wait five minutes for a serving of popcorn? Come on, Addy, that's ridiculous."

We walked toward the toilets together and I wondered what Justin wanted to achieve with this stunt. As if he really had to pee. Come on! It was a cheap ploy to be alone with me.

"Addy," he said as we came to a standstill in front of the toilet block.

"Justin."

I crossed my arms in front of my chest.

"Remember how you promised me you'd be my plus one to the wedding? I still need a suit. Will you come shopping with me tomorrow? There's also a party later that day. Nothing big, just a couple of my friends celebrating a birthday."

I blew a raspberry. "Shopping? Some people have to work during the day."

His face fell and he threw me a disappointed smile.

"Okay, I understand."

He wasn't going to even try and convince me?

He walked to the men's bathroom. Before I could reason with myself, I said, "I'll see if I can arrange something. But I won't know until tomorrow, so no promises."

He stood still for a moment, and since he had his back toward me, I couldn't tell whether he was smiling or not, but I hoped he was.

"Great. Make sure you wear something helicopter-proof," he said, then disappeared into the men's bathroom.

I didn't move an inch, though, as I was too dumbfounded. All I could think about were the words *helicopter-proof*, and whether or not it was one of his silly jokes.

I guessed there was only one way to find out.

CHAPTER THIRTEEN

"And you're sure he said helicopter, not lobster?" Suzie asked, riffling through the pile of clothes on my bed.

I had called her first thing in the morning, asking her to come over to help me with an emergency. The emergency being me needing an outfit to go shopping and partying with Justin.

"Lobster?" I asked. "What would lobster-proof even mean? I'm one hundred percent positive that he said helicopter-proof."

Suzie shrugged. "Maybe he wants you to wear one of those lobster bibs they hand out at seafood restaurants."

I laughed. "I'm not wearing a bib to meet Justin."

"You're right. Maybe put one in your purse, just in case,"

she said. "I'll run next door and ask Alex to give me one."

I held out a dress for her to assess. "The bib can wait. What do you think of this dress?"

She tapped her chin. "Put it in the maybe pile."

I threw the dress down and went through my other clothes.

"So, are you excited Justin asked you to go with him?" Suzie asked.

I shrugged. "It's nice."

"Nice? Come on, Addy. One of the world's hottest movie stars has asked you on a date and all you have to say about it is *nice*?"

I sat down on the bed. "To be honest, I don't know what to feel. Am I attracted to him? I think so. Yesterday, during the movie screening, his toe touched mine and I almost exploded. The real question is, do I like him?"

"I know you two share an unpleasant history, but even I can see that he's fond of you," Suzie said. "Are you… afraid he'll hurt you again?"

I bit my lip. "Maybe. I can't even think about that. My last relationship was messy, and I don't want to put myself through something like that again."

Suzie smiled at me. "Addy. You once told me to take a risk and follow my heart, remember? And look how that turned out. I have the most amazing husband I could've ever wished for."

"I'm sure his yoga experience comes as a great plus in other areas as well," I said with a giggle.

She grinned. "Can't argue with that. But enough about

me. We've only got an hour before Justin is picking you up. Do you still have that dress you bought for the Snow Ball two years ago?"

I went through the pile of clothes on my bed. "I do."

"Why don't you wear that one?"

I unzipped the garment bag. "I don't know. It's way too fancy. It's even got tiny rhinestones and a sash. That's not the kind of thing you'd wear for a helicopter flight."

"Yeah, and also not for a lobster dinner."

"Although, the bib you're forcing me to take would cover most of it anyway," I said with a laugh.

In the end, I settled for a knee-length dress with a lace overlay and paired it with a pair of blue pumps. It was a purely practical decision. Justin probably bought his suits at one of those fancy stores that had a strict no denim and sneakers policy.

Suzie and I exchanged our goodbyes after she insisted I shove a bib in my purse, and I walked toward the inn's parking lot. Justin was leaning against his car, checking something on his phone.

He was dressed in brown leather shoes, suit pants with a dark belt, and a fitted shirt that probably cost more than I made in a month. The sunglasses on his face were too much to handle, though. They made my heart pound so fast I was afraid I might have a heart attack.

I coughed to make him aware of my presence and he looked up. He slid his shades down an inch or two, and a big smile made his eyes light up like fireworks on the fourth of July.

"Let's go," he said, pushing himself off his car and opening the door for me.

I slid into the leather seats, feeling a bit shaky.

Justin walked around the car to get in his own seat. He then gave me a small nod before directing his gaze to the rearview mirror and backing out of his parking space. "You look great."

"You too," I said.

Great was kind of an understatement. Scorching hot was more like it.

"Make yourself comfortable," he said. "It's going to be a while before we get there."

"Oh?" I asked.

He grinned. "Unfortunately, Old Pine Cove doesn't have a suit store yet. At least not the kind I usually shop at."

We spent the hour-long ride to the suit store talking about mundane things, yet the tension between us was unmistakably there the entire time. Like when he put his hand on the gear shift and accidently brushed my leg. Or when I caught him looking at me for a beat too long and I had to snap him out of it before we hit a tree.

I told him about my love for animals, how a petting zoo helped lower people's stress levels, and how I hoped the patch of land next to the inn would be mine soon.

He talked about his favorite baseball team, and how he'd met one of his idols last year.

We happily chatted away, all the while filling the car with sexual tension. It was getting to a point where I needed to crack a window just to let some of it escape. Unfortunately, that didn't help one bit.

By the time Justin pulled into the parking lot of Suits You Well, I was almost panting, desperate to escape the confines of his Tesla.

A big guy in a suit greeted us at the entrance. I'd never had someone greet me at a store before. At least, not someone dressed in fancy evening wear. I had been greeted by a guy in a clown suit once, but that wasn't the kind of suit I was referring to.

"Welcome to Suits You Well, madam," another employee said as we entered the store. "Do you care for a glass of champagne?"

"Why yes, I do," I said.

I didn't know why I sounded like a British septuagenarian all of a sudden. It was most likely the vibes this store sent out. Everything was so classy and expensive. It was hard to wrap my head around the fact that people actually shopped here.

"Do you come here often?" I asked Justin in hushed tones.

"Not here specifically. They have stores all over the country."

The man offering us champagne, who was called Ray according to his nametag, led us to a seating area that looked more like a mansion's living room than part of a store.

A crystal chandelier adorned the roof above our heads, and the leather sofas seemed to be hand-stitched. I let my hand run over the fabric. It probably cost more than all of the furniture in my house.

I was relieved that I had decided on wearing a dress, instead of my usual jeans and shirt outfit.

A woman placed two glasses of champagne on the marble coffee table in front of us. I thanked her before she click-clacked away on her high heels.

"What are your current suit needs, sir?" Ray asked.

Justin and Ray got talking about cuffs, lapels, and colors. Who knew there were so many options when it came to suits?

Justin disappeared into the dressing room to try on one of the suits, handpicked by Ray himself. He opened the curtain a few minutes later.

"What do you think, Addy?" he asked.

"I… uh…"

My ability to think up a sentence had flown right out of the window.

Justin's face fell. "You don't like it, do you?"

"I do," I said.

He was wearing a dark navy suit, a black leather belt making sure that his pants hung snug, yet classy, around his legs and ass. Justin in normal clothes looked amazing, but Justin in a suit? I now completely understood why he always had hordes of women chasing after him, trying to touch him, or even so much as elicit a smile from him.

"Are you sure?" he asked. "You look a bit shocked."

I gulped half of my champagne down. "I am one hundred percent positive. Your nuts look amazing. You. I mean you."

Wow, I had to stop talking about his nuts. A hint of anger flared up inside of me. It was like Justin made me act in a bad way when I was a good girl. Why did he keep doing that?

Or maybe I wasn't as innocent as I believed? What if, deep down, I had a bad side that no other guy had ever been able to trigger?

Justin laughed. "At least you're being honest. I like this one too. Let's try on a couple of others and compare," he said to Ray.

With every suit he put on, I got weaker and dizzier. Looking that good in a suit should be prosecutable. Maybe I should take matters into my own hands and call the FBI to report him. Surely looking irresistible and causing someone to have heart palpitations could technically be considered a crime.

Justin and I picked out two suits, the navy one and a black one, and they altered them for him right then and there. I had never known this kind of service existed, but then again, money could buy you anything. Or so I'd heard people say.

After we were all set, we followed Ray to the register. Justin asked him to deliver the suits to the inn, then got his credit card out of his wallet.

"That'll be eleven thousand dollars and fifty-five cents," Ray said without blinking.

I almost fainted, feeling even dizzier than before. "Eleven thousand dollars?" I cried out.

"It's no big deal," Justin said. "They're quality and they

are comfortable."

Comfortable? My most comfortable outfit was a unicorn onesie that I'd bought for twenty dollars during a sale. Our worlds were clearly miles apart, maybe even planets apart.

We left the store in silence. I was still too shocked by the amount of money Justin had just forked over to string together a conversation.

"Is everything okay?" he asked as soon as we were in his sexual-tension-filled car again.

I nodded. "Everything's a-okay." I gave him a thumbs-up.

"Good. I'm not used to you being this quiet."

I turned in my seat to face him. "Justin, I've got to ask. Are we going to get into a helicopter, or are we having a lobster dinner?"

"I did plan on taking a helicopter to that party I told you about, yes. The lobster dinner? I don't know. I guess there will be lobster, but I'm not sure. Why?"

My heart did a double take and I pushed the lobster bib deeper into my purse. I was going to fly in a helicopter. A real one, not the ones they have at amusement parks.

"No reason," I said, beaming. "What kind of party is this anyway? I said yes before you even shared the details."

He followed the highway signs leading to the airport. "It's a small get-together with some of my colleagues."

"Your colleagues. As in, *In Dire Need* colleagues?"

He nodded. "That's right. It's Alicia's birthday."

I gasped. "Alicia Bright is having a birthday party and

I'm invited?"

Justin laughed. "Yes. She's at her house in Boston at the moment. It's only a couple of hours by helicopter. You're not going to act all funny around these people, are you? Or steal their snacks?"

His expression had gone from amused to concerned.

I shook my head. "No, no, no. I'm going to act absolutely normal and I'll only eat what is served. I won't rummage through their cabinets."

Granted, my current behavior didn't bode well for Justin, but come on. I was going to Alicia Bright's birthday party. In a helicopter! If I didn't know any better, I'd think Ray had drugged me with that glass of champagne.

I got my phone out and texted Suzie to tell her that I wasn't going to attend a lobster dinner after all, but a celebrity birthday party. Not to mention going on an actual helicopter ride.

She immediately texted me back. "WHAT?! IS THIS A JOKE, ADDY?"

I assured her it wasn't a joke, and I'd send pictures later. Then I made a quick call to Carter. I needed to know if he had everything under control at the inn, or I wouldn't be able to enjoy myself, no matter how over the top this evening was going to be. Thankfully, everything was okay at the inn.

When Justin stopped the car at the airport, I couldn't believe my eyes. A shiny black helicopter towered before us, the blades whizzing away.

Some guy in a suit approached us and held the car door

open.

"Are you ready for this?" Justin asked with a grin.

"You bet I am," I said.

We got out of the car and walked toward the helicopter, me with a spring in my step. This was going to be such a fun ride.

CHAPTER FOURTEEN

The Maine landscape fell away behind us as we set a course for Boston for Alicia's birthday party. I had to pinch myself a couple of times to make sure I wasn't dreaming.

Justin on the other hand was as relaxed as could be. This was probably not his first time in a helicopter. I was a tad nervous, though, and hoped that disaster wouldn't strike.

I tried to steer my thoughts away from plummeting to my death and redirected them to the party. It hit me that I didn't have a gift. How rude was that? Then again, I didn't even know it was a celebrity's birthday party up until half an hour ago.

Who was I kidding? There was no excuse for not bringing a birthday present to a party, not in my book anyway.

"We didn't bring a gift," I said into my headset.

Justin turned toward me and casually put a hand on my leg. "Don't worry, I've got it covered."

I stared at his hand, trying to figure out what it was doing there. Then I reminded myself of all the reasons I hated him, but hardly any came to mind. All I knew was he made my heart skip a beat whenever he was around me, and at night in my dreams.

He followed my gaze and pulled his hand away. "I'm sorry, I know you don't like that."

He peered out of the window again. His suit pants touched the bare skin of my leg, and my brain flooded with confusing thoughts.

Why was I on this flight? Why me specifically? Justin could've asked anyone to come with him, and yet he asked me. Did that mean he... liked me? I couldn't wrap my head around that idea. For years he had teased me, made my high school years a true struggle, and now he was all "oh, let's go on a helicopter ride and attend Alicia Bright's birthday party together. And while we're at it, why don't I touch your leg and have my gorgeous smile make you melt into a confused puddle?"

Ugh. And they say women are hard to read. It's men who should come with a user manual.

Relief washed over me when we finally touched solid ground again. It had been an amazing experience, but I needed to put a tiny bit of space between the two of us. That helicopter was way too small to contain me and my feelings for Justin.

We stepped into the evening air, a soft breeze playing with the hem of my dress. Justin put his hand on the small of my back and led me to a sleek sports car that had been waiting for us. The driver opened the door, and we both slid into the leather seats.

"So, you got Alicia something from the both of us?" I asked as the car whizzed through traffic.

"I did. We won't show up empty-handed, so stop worrying."

I threw him a look.

"What?" he asked.

"I can't know what we're giving her?" I asked, raising an eyebrow.

He laughed. "That's not what I said. You asked me if I had bought her something, not what it was that I'd bought."

I sighed dramatically. "Stuff like this is exactly why I go back and forth between liking and hating you."

He grinned and his eyes started twinkling. "You like me. I told you I'd prove you wrong."

"I said like *and* hate. That's not the same as full-on liking you. The jury is still out on that one. I can guarantee you the scale will tip back to full-on hating if you keep acting this silly."

He handed me a cream-colored envelope. "If you must know, I got her a voucher to go bungee jumping."

I let out a laugh. "That's it?"

He ran a hand through his hair. "Yes. Why?"

"No reason," I said with a shrug, and handed him the

envelope back. "It just seems a bit cheap. Especially after spending eleven thousand dollars on a suit."

"Two suits. And for the record, just because we're actors doesn't mean we go buying private islands for each other's birthdays. We're all still normal people."

I grinned at him. "I wouldn't call you normal, but okay."

He turned toward me, his arms crossed over his chest. "What do you think I should've gotten her?"

Ah. Such a good question, yet I didn't have a satisfying answer. "I don't hang out with celebrities," I said. "I don't know what they like. A thousand bottles of expensive champagne maybe?"

Justin cocked an eyebrow, then burst out laughing. "What would someone even do with a thousand bottles of champagne? I don't want to give her alcohol poisoning."

I felt my cheeks burn and turned my head to look out of the window. "Duh, drink them. Share them with friends. Like I said, I don't know."

"Hey, don't be mad," he said, his voice softer than before. "I appreciate you putting in your two cents. We could stop and get her a bottle of champagne if that would make you happy."

I uncrossed my arms and sighed. "That's okay. I think I'm nervous. I want to make a good impression."

He threw me a warm smile. "You'll make a great impression."

"Thanks."

The taxi pulled into a broad driveway, and Alicia's enormous house came into view. I expected her to live in some fancy villa, but I hadn't imagined something this huge.

"Sweet mother of cookie dough," I said, pushing my face against the car window to get an even better view and soak up every detail.

My own house could fit into hers twenty times over and then some. The driveway was filled with shiny, expensive cars, and the path leading to the front door was adorned with gold and pink balloon arrangements.

Justin thanked our driver, then hurried around the car to open my door. With every step we took toward the house, the music and laughter coming from inside grew louder, and so did the nervous beating of my heart. Didn't Justin say this was going to be a small birthday party? It sure didn't sound like it.

The door swung open before Justin could even lift his finger off the doorbell. Standing before us was Alicia Bright, in the flesh. Or, well, in a bohemian dress that looked more like a large fitted shirt. The garment barely reached to her thighs. On me it would've looked ridiculous, but it looked gorgeous on her. Leather sandals with straps made of colorful beads wrapped all around her ankles.

A big smile spread across her face and she pulled Justin in for a hug. "Jussie! You made it!"

Jussie? I had to stifle a laugh.

"And who is this pretty girl?" she asked, her eyes sparkling with delight.

He smiled at me. "This is Addy. We've known each other for years."

She hugged me with the same beaming smile she had

given Justin. "Welcome, Addy."

"I hope you don't mind me bringing someone along," Justin said.

Alicia waved his remark away. "Nonsense, Addy is more than welcome here. I think it's great you finally brought a date to one of my parties. Now, come on, don't just stand there on the doorstep. The party's this way."

We followed her inside. Justin didn't even try to correct her when she said I was his date. Did that mean this was indeed a date? I thought it was me doing him a favor, because he didn't want to go alone. I stole a glance at him, but nothing gave away that he was freaked out about this being a date.

I decided to concentrate on other things, like— Oh, tiny appetizers. A waiter carrying a tray of shrimp and mango sauce offered me one, and I gladly accepted. I hadn't eaten anything for hours.

Justin weaved through the crowd, until we got to the bar that was set up on the patio. Pink inflatable flamingos and a bunch of imported palm trees gave the backyard a tropical feel. I could get used to parties like these.

"Miller, you're here," someone with a familiar voice said.

I turned around and had to do my best to contain myself. Russell Grey, Oscar nominated actor, fist-bumped Justin. Then he extended his hand to shake mine.

"Nice to meet you, sir," I said.

Russell laughed. "Sir? Please, call me Russell."

I almost asked him for a selfie with me. The words were on the tip of my tongue, but I held it together and swallowed them back down. I didn't want to be known as a star-crazed girl, and I was positive everyone here was glad to get away from the attention for once.

"How do you and Justin know each other?" he asked, popping an olive in his mouth.

"We grew up in the same town," Justin said. "She pretends to hate me, but she's nuts about me. Actually, she's also nuts about nuts."

"Don't flatter yourself, Kermit," I said, then turned to Russell. "This one made sure my high school years were quite hellish. He went out of his way to make fun of me every chance he got."

Justin crossed his arms. "Did not."

I turned back to Russell. "He did. Also, I'm hardly nuts about *Jussie* over here. I tolerate him."

"She'll like me after she sees what I've got planned," Justin told Russell, ignoring me.

Russell grinned. "Man, this is going to be such an interesting night."

The two of them started talking about work, call times, and scripts. Meanwhile, the cogs in my head kept turning. Justin had planned something, and I didn't like it one bit. What if me coming here was all some ploy to make fun of me? I still wasn't one hundred percent sure about trusting him.

I pushed my worries aside. All I'd been doing lately was worry. Tonight was about having a good time. So what if Justin had planned something stupid? I was here to party with celebs. Nothing could ruin that experience.

I ordered myself a glass of champagne and plucked another appetizer from a passing tray. The food at this party was next level. Alicia probably had a private chef that catered to her every need. It was quite an accomplishment that she was able to stay so thin. If I had a private chef, I'd never stop eating.

As I sipped my drink and munched on my food, I let my gaze wander around the room. It was weird seeing all these people I knew from TV in real life. They looked exactly like they did on the small screen, yet completely different at the same time.

Then Justin put his hand on the small of my back, guiding me inside. "Alicia's about to make a speech," he said.

"Uh-huh."

His hand didn't leave its spot, and I felt my face go beetroot. *Relax,* I told myself. *Breathe.*

Alicia grabbed a microphone and thanked everyone for coming. She said some other things as well, but I didn't hear one word of it. Justin's hand was still on my back, turning my extremities into Jell-O.

The applause that went around the room snapped me out of the blubbering state I was in. Justin leaned closer, his lips brushing against my ear.

Every hair on my body shot up when he whispered, "You think you hate me? I'm going to prove you wrong, Addy. You long for me, and you know it."

Then he let go. He walked over to Alicia with confident strides and took the microphone from her. A grin unfurled across his mouth as he slung a guitar around his body.

"I know this guitar belongs to the band who's going to perform later, but they were nice enough to let me borrow it. I've got something special prepared for tonight, friends."

His gaze zoomed in on me and he winked. He rolled his sleeves up to his elbows, and the sight of his strong forearms made me gasp. I needed another drink. My throat had become as dry as a desert.

"I wrote this one myself, so please bear with me. It's far from perfect, but I hope it'll do the trick."

Justin strummed the guitar, eliciting cheers from the crowd. My eyes were transfixed on his mouth, his fingers forming the chords, his expression nothing but lust-inducing. I put a hand over my mouth, nearly hyperventilating.

"Let me melt your icy heart," he sang, his voice reverberating through the room. "I know you love to hate me, and it's driving me insane."

He looked at me, and I could feel everyone else's eyes on me as well. This made zero sense. Was he… doing this for me? Why?

I backed away and ran. I couldn't bear to hear what he was going to sing about next. I pushed through the crowd and opened the first door I could find.

I knew that running away was lame and that I'd have to stop doing it sooner or later, but for now, I figured later would do the trick. As long as I kept pushing the truth away, it wouldn't be real, would it?

Oh, who was I kidding. The truth was undeniable. It was right there in my sweaty palms, my pounding heart, and elevated body temperature.

I needed something to fan myself with, or I'd faint. I let my gaze wander to find something useful, but apparently, I had stumbled into a pantry.

Still, I wasn't going to let someone find me unconscious at Alicia Bright's birthday party. I ripped open a package of lasagna sheets and fanned myself with one of them.

There were footsteps outside, and someone rattled the doorknob. Justin came bursting in, his forearms still bare, taunting my insides to light on fire.

He stared at the lasagna sheet in my hand. It was enough to make his scowl disappear. "What are you doing?"

I swallowed. "I needed some air."

He closed the door behind him, taking a cautious step toward me. I didn't back away this time.

"You didn't like the song?" His voice came out low and hoarse.

"I did. It was good," I said, barely audible.

He was now so close that our faces were only inches apart. His blue eyes were about to swallow me whole and his manly scent filled the entire pantry. "Then why did you run away?"

Oh my God. Someone must've spiked my drink. This was one of those things you read about in magazines. There simply wasn't any other explanation, because I wanted to push Justin against a wall and kiss him in a way that would make him forget he'd ever kissed another girl.

"Addy?"

I blinked. "What?"

He shook his head. "What's a guy got to do, Addy? Besides building a fence for your duck, taking you on helicopter rides, and performing a song at a party. What?"

"I… I don't know what you're talking about."

Still locking eyes with me, he let his fingers travel down my arm and grabbed my hand. The lasagna sheet clattered to the ground.

"You know exactly what I'm talking about, Addison Grant."

CHAPTER FIFTEEN

My inner voice screamed at me to tell him I liked him, but I couldn't form any words.

Justin stopped speaking as well. Now we were two silent people locked in a pantry, staring at each other, breathing way too loud and fast. This was getting dangerous. Any more of this and the scale would tip. I couldn't let that happen, or I'd be a goner.

"I guess I'm…" I started.

"Yes?"

I let my tongue run over my lips as I searched for the appropriate words. "I'm waiting for the other shoe to drop."

His brow furrowed. "What other shoe? There are no shoes and none of them are going to drop."

"How can I be sure?" I asked.

He shook his head and balled his free hand into a fist. "I've had enough of playing games. When you're ready, come and find me."

He let go of my hand, turned around, and walked out.

This was the part where I was supposed to go after him, no? Instead, I was frozen in place. My hands were shaking so badly I had to grab a shelf to steady myself. The realization that maybe I did like him, way more than I wanted to admit to myself, had shocked me to my core.

Now what? I couldn't hide in this pantry forever, but I couldn't go out there and mingle either. Justin was the only person I really knew at this party.

I decided to wait half an hour before showing my face again. Since I was still hungry, I cracked open a bag of tortilla chips and a jar of dip.

I slid to the floor and put a chip into the cheese dip. This was pathetic. There was a party on the other side of that door, with shrimp, puffy pastries, and grilled salmon. Not to mention famous people. And I was stuffing my face with ordinary chips in someone's pantry. I couldn't believe I had let it come this far.

A tear fell down my face, and I got my phone out of my purse to text Suzie.

"I like him. I need help," I typed, then erased the message again. There was no use sending my feelings out into the world like that. What would Suzie be able to do about it? This was all on me. There was only one thing I could do, and that was talk to Justin.

Running away from the most romantic thing anyone

had ever done for me had been a major mistake. It wasn't fair to Justin at all, but his trying to sweep me off my feet had come completely out of the blue.

I trembled as I thought about the significance of his gesture. Justin Miller liked me enough to sing me a song in front of all those people.

I wiped my hands on a paper towel. Then I took a deep breath before opening the door, and slipped into the party again.

It didn't take me long to spot Justin. He was standing near the sliding doors that led to the patio. He'd lost the tie and had unbuttoned his shirt a bit so that his chest was showing. Next to him was a man I didn't recognize. Maybe I wasn't the only person here who didn't star in some show or movie after all.

Okay. I needed to go over there and talk to him. That couldn't be too hard. I might need some liquid courage, though. And some solid courage as well.

I downed a glass of champagne and when the waiter wasn't looking, I grabbed another one.

There. Now I was ready.

I zoomed in on my target and approached him. When I was close enough, I cleared my throat. "Excuse me, can we talk?"

Justin's eyes nervously flicked between me and the man he was talking to. "I'll be right over. Why don't I meet you outside in five?"

"Perfect," I said, and took my breadsticks with hummus dip outside.

I positioned myself on one of the loungers next to the pool. The spot gave me a great view of Justin, who kept glancing at me with a suspicious expression on his face.

That's right, Kermit the Frog, I'm going to tell you something you'd never thought possible.

A couple of minutes later, Justin shook the man's hand and gave him a curt nod. Finally, he was on his way to me. I sat up straight, my palms clammy from the anticipation of what was about to go down.

"What's up?" Justin asked.

It was like nothing had happened between us. How could he remain so cool? Then again, he was an actor, which meant he was probably an expert at hiding his true emotions.

I patted the spot beside me. "Come and sit."

He reluctantly sat down. His arms were crossed, which only drew attention to his unbuttoned shirt. Did he really need to shove that delicious ripped chest in my face right now?

"Jussie, is this a date?" I asked.

Instead of answering, he countered with a question. "Are you drunk?"

I blew out a puff of air and pointed a bread stick at him. "Just answer the question, Jussie."

"You are. You're drunk. When did this happen?"

I frowned. I wasn't intoxicated. Maybe a bit, yes, but not *drunk* drunk. "I. Am. Not."

"Well, I can't tell for sure. And that means that I can't have this conversation with you. Not when you might say things you'll regret later."

This was ludicrous. First, he was mad because I ran and hid inside a pantry, and now he didn't want to talk to me when I made it crystal clear that I finally wanted to? Men! Unbelievable.

My nostrils flared at this unfairness. "Fine. We won't talk."

"Maybe we should go home," he said. "This entire night has been a disaster from start to finish."

"But we haven't even had cake yet. You can't do this to me. I'm sure Alicia will have ordered the best cake ever."

"Cake? That's what you're concerned about?"

I got up, ready to run, but then realized I had nowhere to run to. Unlike Justin, I didn't have a helicopter on standby that I could summon whenever I wanted to.

I plopped back down into my seat. "Whatever. We can't go. It's rude to leave a party this early and I hate rudeness. You should know that by now."

"Fine."

He turned his head away, his gaze anywhere except on me.

"Maybe we should do something that doesn't involve any talking," I said. "I heard someone mention a foosball table in the entertainment room. Can you believe Alicia's got an entertainment room? My living room is hardly big enough to fit a television, and she's got an entire space dedicated to—"

Justin spun his head back in my direction. "You're babbling. I thought we weren't going to talk."

I got up and threw him an expectant look. "Shall we go find that foosball table?"

He got up as well, so slow that he looked like a ninety-year-old man with knee and back problems. His mouth was a hard line. Had I broken his playfulness? I didn't like his change in behavior, even though I couldn't blame him. I owed him an apology for sure, but I also needed time to process my thoughts and feelings.

The entertainment room was located in the basement. A fancy one, not the *someone's going to get murdered here* type of basement. The room was light and airy, and a comfortable-looking couch sat on a shag carpet. A giant subwoofer and different game consoles were set up against one of the walls.

"Are we playing, or are you going to keep drooling over those game consoles?" Justin asked.

I took my place at the other side of the foosball table, and we let our miniature players kick the ball without either of us uttering a word.

On the outside, I looked normal. I hoped. But on the inside, I couldn't catch up. How had I gone from being in a suit store to having feelings for this gorgeous guy who was now kicking a tiny ball with such force that I was scared he'd break the entire table?

Did I *really* have feelings for him? After all, there was a thin line between love and hate. It was true that I was warming up to him, and that he set my skin ablaze whenever he touched me, but that didn't mean I wanted to marry him and have his babies.

Justin let out a low groan when the ball whizzed right past his goalkeeper. I tallied up the numbers.

"I'm winning," I said. I felt oddly proud of that achievement.

"I thought we weren't going to talk?"

He stared me down. Again. How many more times was he going to do that?

"Why not? I feel it's time to talk."

He opened his mouth, and I leaned in. I needed to hear what he was about to say. He furrowed his brows and sighed.

"Do you mind?" he said, turning his head toward the door where Russell had materialized. Talk about having impeccable timing.

"Sorry to interrupt," Russell said. "Alicia's about to cut the cake and she wants everyone there."

Justin turned to me again, a smirk on his face. "Well, seems like you won't miss the cake after all."

He joined Russell by the door and the three of us walked back to the living room. Justin left me alone, greeting some more people. Whatever. I didn't need him to have fun.

I focused my attention on the enormous flamingo cake that was on a table. It had six layers, all pink and golden. On top of the cake was a marzipan flamingo that looked too cute to eat. Still, I'd put it in my mouth first chance.

Alicia posed for pictures, then cut the cake while everyone was singing Happy Birthday. I snapped a couple of pictures myself and sent them to Suzie.

Since Justin was nowhere to be seen, I took my slice

of cake outside. A waiter stopped by my side and offered me another glass of champagne. He probably felt sorry for me, eating all by myself. I thanked him, but declined. I didn't need any more alcohol. What I needed was clarity.

I found a secluded spot at the back of the yard and sat down in the grass, my back against a tree and my legs stretched out in front of me. I kicked off my shoes, and took a bite of the cake, not even bothering to use a fork. I gobbled down the entire slice in only five bites. Yes, it was very unladylike, but come on. This was no ordinary cake. It must've been laced with flavor-enhancing bits. Or made by some famous chef.

I closed my eyes, trying to fight off the confusing thoughts I had about Justin. It was all too exhausting to deal with right now.

Sleep might help. I could forget about everything and just let some weird dream take over my thoughts.

I had almost drifted off into a blissful nap when a small object landed in my lap. I jumped to my feet, afraid of finding a giant spider or some other creepy creature.

"Why do I always find you asleep with some type of food attached to you?"

Justin was standing a couple of feet away from me, looking all amused.

"Did you just throw something at me?"

He picked up a small packet from the grass and handed it to me.

"What's this?" I asked, even though it was clear that Justin had thrown a packet of peanuts into my lap as if I was a circus monkey.

"Food for the flight back home. You should eat, or you'll get nauseous on the helicopter."

I cocked an eyebrow. "I thought you told me not to steal anything at this party?"

"Well, Alicia's my friend. She won't mind that I took some nuts to help my drunk friend."

"First of all, I'm not drunk. And second… are we? Friends, I mean?"

My hands started shaking simply from asking that question.

Justin took a step closer. "We might have a weird way of interacting with each other, but I'd say we are friends. That does mean you have to stop pretending to hate me. I know it's all an act. You can't fool me by saying you don't feel the tension between us."

"Tension?" I asked.

"Like before, in the car," he said.

My heart was about to leap out of my throat. I hadn't imagined it. He had felt it too.

He leaned in and let his fingers brush against mine. "Or when I do this."

I closed my eyes. To hell with all my rules, and the fact that Justin had hurt me years ago. He stepped on stage for me in front of his friends and colleagues. I wanted to kiss him so badly, but at the same time, fear crept up on me. What if he wasn't being genuine? And if he was, then how would I ever be good enough for him? He lived this amazing celebrity lifestyle, and I was just a small-town girl.

I had to start taking chances. I had to start living it up. If that meant getting kissed at a celebrity birthday party by a guy who made me feel all conflicted, bring it on. It didn't have to mean anything, just some good old-fashioned fun, right?

But nothing was being brought on. My lips were not being kissed.

"Justin, I'm sorry. About before. I shouldn't have run away. I panicked," I said.

He gave me a nod, then turned around.

"Our ride is here," Justin said. "Are you coming? It's time to head back to Old Pine Cove. Oh, and there's some cake sticking to your cheek. You might want to wipe that off first."

And just like that, my feet got planted firmly on the ground again.

CHAPTER SIXTEEN

The next couple of days, I wanted nothing more than to scream, "What does it all mean?" I couldn't, of course. The inn guests would think I was certifiable for sure.

Every time I ran into Justin – which happened only three times, to be exact – he stared me down. We hadn't spoken in days and it was starting to annoy me. Luckily, the wedding preparations took up most of my time, so I didn't have to think about what happened at the birthday party all the time.

Layla had even invited me to her bachelorette party, despite the fact that we didn't know each other that well. She said she was immensely grateful that I was dealing with all the wedding prep, and wanted me to feel included. I think she secretly meant she was elated she didn't have to work on her wedding with Diane breathing down her neck. I could deal with the neck-breathing knowing it was only temporary, but poor Layla had a lifetime of Diane's meddling to look forward to.

Diane had asked me the day before to provide some extra space at the wedding to sell her vacuum cleaners. I kindly told her I didn't think selling vacuum cleaners at her grandson's wedding was appropriate, but she argued about it in true Diane fashion.

Going to Layla's bachelorette party would be a nice interlude from Diane's demands, so I'd gladly accepted.

At four, I left the inn. We would all be meeting outside of Sip'nBean before picking up Layla.

I didn't know what Layla's friends had planned, but I hoped it would be something decent. I wasn't in the mood to peel off some stripper's underwear with my teeth. Not that I was ever in the mood to do that, mind you.

I had my hand on the doorknob of the coffee shop when I saw a girl running toward me. "Am I too late? My boss wouldn't let me go one minute earlier."

She put her hands on her knees, out of breath. Frankly, she looked as if she'd run from a city office all the way to Old Pine Cove.

"I don't think you're late. It's only quarter past four," I said. "I'm Addy, by the way."

"Stella," the girl said in between breaths. "Nice to meet you."

The door swung open and four other girls spilled out of

the building. "The limo should be here any minute," one them of said. "We decided to wait outside."

"Is everyone here?" a short brunette asked, looking around the group of girls.

I caught a glimpse of Suzie and gladly joined her. Since Layla was a regular at Suzie's bookstore, she had been invited as well.

"There," the brunette shouted.

A shiny white limousine came into view and stopped right next to us. A girl jumped out and yelled, "Who's ready to party?"

The others – except for me, Suzie, and Olive – jumped up and down, all screaming in delight.

"And guess what I brought with me," the limo girl shouted.

She waved around a giant inflatable red guitar that looked like a crooked penis. What was she planning on doing with that? For a second, I thought about feigning some rare illness, but I couldn't do that to the others. Everything had been planned and I didn't want to be a party pooper.

We all climbed into the limo and Stella proposed an introductory round, as we didn't all know each other yet.

The inflatable guitar girl was called Ashley. She'd met Layla in college. The short brunette was Brianna, one of Layla's colleagues, and the other girl was called Jess. She worked as a sales rep for organic food for farm chickens, ducks, and geese. What that meant, I didn't know, but she was extremely passionate about it. When I told her I had a duck and was planning on opening a petting zoo next to the inn, she shoved a business card in my hands, telling me to call her as soon as the deal to buy the land was done. Then she got out a bottle of hand sanitizer and squirted some of the liquid on her hands.

"The eight of us are going to have so much fun today," Ashley said, the inflatable toy now at her feet.

I hoped she was right.

"If I ever meet someone and get married, I'll make you regret it if you dare bring me something like that," I said to Suzie, pointing at the inflatable toy. "It looks like a faulty penis."

"You have to admit, it's a bit funny," Suzie whispered.

I giggled. "Maybe a little bit, yes. As long as I don't have to touch it, I'm good."

The limo stopped once again, this time to pick up Layla. The girls ordered her to strap the penis guitar around her body and popped a bottle of champagne.

Oh boy. At least Layla didn't look uncomfortable, or she was good at pretending. There was no way to tell.

"So, where are we headed first?" Olive asked. "Or is that a secret?"

Ashley wiggled her eyebrows suggestively. "You'll see. But I can promise you girls it's something good."

The limo exited Old Pine Cove, and my thoughts swiveled back to that night when Justin and I left town. I felt dizzy thinking about the look he had given me when he played me that song. Damn, why hadn't I stayed and listened to it?

"Addy over here partied with celebs a few days ago,"

Olive said.

"What?" Brianna called out. "Who? Do you have pictures? Tell us everything!"

She grabbed my shoulders and pleaded with me as if I was a drug dealer and she was running low on heroine.

"It was just a birthday party," I said.

I didn't feel like sharing details about my night with Justin. It was something between him and me, and now the world knew about it. Well, maybe not the world, but several other girls. Everyone knew that meant it was only a matter of time before word spread far and wide.

"We need more details than that," Ashley said.

Layla shot me a smile. "You went with Justin, right?"

I nodded. "That's right. He's an old friend."

"I almost forgot you guys share a hometown with Justin Miller," Ashley said. "He's so gorgeous. Is he going to be at the wedding?"

"He's Asher's best man," Layla said, adjusting the inflatable instrument that was strapped around her body.

The others got all dreamy-eyed. Ashley even had to fan herself. "I wonder if he's still single. I would kill to go out with a guy like that." Then she turned to me. "Addy, since Justin's an old friend, why don't you introduce us?"

She wanted me to do what now?

"Err… I don't know. We're not that close."

Brianna frowned. "But you went to a party with him?"

Thank goodness Suzie cut in. "It's complicated. Anyway, this day isn't about Addy or Justin Miller, right? How about a small clue as to where we're headed?"

Ashley took the bait and I threw Suzie a grateful smile for directing the conversation somewhere else.

I peered at Ashley, feeling not so fond of her. Who did she think she was, wanting me to set her up with Justin? She didn't even know him – apart from how ridiculously high his score on the hotness meter was.

I didn't want to act all jealous and I knew Justin wasn't mine. I just couldn't help myself.

I spent the rest of the ride trying to take part in the conversation, but it was hard to focus on anything when I knew that others had their arrows pointed at Justin.

Forty-five minutes later, the limo pulled into the parking lot of a fancy-looking building. A big sign read *Cloverleaf Spa & Wellness.*

We got out of the limo and Ashley took the lead. She walked to the entrance with confident strides, as opposed to Layla who was trying to hide the fact that she had a giant penis-looking toy strapped around her body.

We all stepped through the sliding doors, entering a haven of tranquility. A small fountain surrounded by all kinds of jungle plants stood in the center of the lobby. Soft ambient music consisting of nature sounds drifted out of the speakers and sunlight poured in through the giant glass roof.

Ashley spun on her heel and clapped her hands. "We're going to get manicures, pedicures, and a makeover," she said with a squeal. "We want to look all pretty for the… rougher activity I have planned later today."

The group fell silent at the mention of a rougher activity. I couldn't blame them for feeling anxious about what that meant, but then again, how bad could it be? Even swimming would be considered an activity rougher than getting manicures.

A lady dressed in white welcomed us to the spa, handing us all a glass of cucumber water. "If you would follow me," she said, leading us to a changing room decked out with plush sofas and personalized slippers.

"Before the manicures, we've got a mud bath prepared for you," the lady said. "You will have to take off that thing, though," she said, glancing at the red penis guitar.

"Not a problem." Layla ripped the toy off as if it was on fire and tossed it on one of the sofas. "There, all set."

The lady smiled at us. "Great, please head to treatment room B as soon as you're ready."

After she left, Jess pointed to the personalized slippers. "I'm not putting those on my feet," she said, armes crossed in front of her chest like a sulky child. The only thing that was missing was her stamping her feet in protest.

"Why not?" Brianna asked.

She scoffed. "Seriously? There could be bacteria on them. It's unsanitary."

"They're unused," Ashley said, stripping down and slipping her feet into her slippers before putting on her robe.

Jess let out a high-pitched laugh. "Yeah, that's what they want you to believe."

"For god's sake, Jess, just put them on. They're wrapped in plastic and there's a label that says *single-person use only* on them. Believe me, they are new."

"So you say, but there's no way to be one hundred percent sure, is there?"

Ashley sighed. "I'm ninety-nine percent sure and that's enough for me. Let's just go and enjoy our mud bath, okay?"

"You know how Jess's anxiety flares up when something like this happens," Layla said, trying to calm down the bickering girls. "Maybe she can stay in the lobby while we slide into those mud baths."

Ashley put a hand on her hip. "This place is the most hygienic one in the state. That's why I booked it. If Jess wants to be a party pooper, fine, but don't say I didn't try to cater to her needs."

Jess let out a puff of air and rolled her eyes. "Fine, you're right. I'll give it a shot."

The eight of us walked out of the changing room, all looking perfectly normal. Jess was wearing socks in her slippers, her fingers tightly clasped around a family-sized bottle of hand sanitizer.

A brightly smiling girl in a white-and-green uniform led us to a big space. Marble tubs filled to the brim with volcanic mud were placed in the center of the room, separated from each other by a wooden end table where a glass of champagne was awaiting each of us.

"The mud bath is about 100 degrees, so you'll be nice and comfortable," the girl said.

After she told us what to expect from this treatment, I took off my robe, sat myself on the edge, and flung myself in, feet first. Instead of sinking into the mud, as I had thought would happen, I lay on top of it and was suddenly very aware of how exposed I was. It wasn't like the others didn't know what a naked woman's body looked like, but I'd rather not have them spot my nether regions. Luckily, the mud-bath attendant came to my rescue, wrapping the thick mud around my body with swift precision.

Once I was settled in the mud, I took a bite of the strawberry that floated around in my champagne and closed my eyes. I could get used to this. Would it be difficult to install one of these at home? Or at work? Now that would be amazing.

I had almost drifted into some peaceful meditative state when Jess started talking.

"This can't be normal. Is this normal? Hello?" she called out. Oh no, she wasn't having another one of her anxiety attacks, was she?

Ashley turned her head around, and shot Jess an encouraging smile. "Just relax. I'm sure everything is normal."

"It's not. Why is no one coming? Can't they hear us? What if there's a fire?" she shouted.

"A fire?" Brianna asked, her brows furrowed.

Jess flailed around in the mud, then put a hand to her chest. "This mud is so heavy, I can't breathe. Can you guys breathe?"

"Yes, I can breathe totally fine," Stella said. "Getting yourself worked up is only going to make you feel worse, Jess."

"I need to get out of here." Her eyes shot from the door to us and back again. "Why isn't anyone coming?"

She was right though. Why wasn't anyone coming? Surely, they must be able to hear the crazy screams coming from treatment room B?

I put my champagne glass down. "I'm sure someone will come to help you real soon."

"Yeah, try to relax," Ashley said.

"Relax?" she shouted, as if someone had just suggested she should eat a plate of broken glass. "I'm not having this, you know, I'm getting out."

"Please, calm down," Brianna said.

Of course, Jess wasn't calmed down by Brianna telling her to calm down.

She put both hands on the side of the tub and lifted herself up, the mud slowly dripping down and falling to the ground with nasty thuds, revealing her birthday suit inch by inch. She grabbed a white towel and flung it around her body, then walked to the door with big, wide steps, leaving small puddles of mud behind her. And then she was gone.

CHAPTER SEVENTEEN

After the mud bath fiasco, Jess told us she'd rather watch the seven of us getting a makeover than participate in one. She was afraid of the makeup brushes not being thoroughly washed and containing some nasty bacteria, so she was the only one who didn't take a seat in one of the makeup chairs.

The makeup artists started working, using the dozens of makeup products covering the countertops in front of us. A warm feeling went through me as I thought about how stunning I'd look after this makeover. It felt so good to get pampered for once.

A mere twenty minutes later, my metamorphosis was complete. The salmon-colored lip gloss, the golden highlights right above my eyelids, and the subtle blush on my cheeks worked perfectly together.

I thanked the makeup artist who had made this possible and looked at the others who were also almost done. Everyone chatted about their favorite mascara brands while Jess scrunched her nose at the mere mention of eyeliner.

"Honestly, I don't understand how you can be a rep for poultry food when you're this afraid of touching anything," Ashley said as a makeup artist swept blush onto her cheek. "Don't chickens and ducks carry lots of diseases?"

"I'm a sales rep, Ash. I don't actually need to touch the animals or their food," Jess said.

Layla rolled her eyes and looked at me. "Don't mind them. They're always on each other's backs, but they do love one another. Am I right, guys?"

"Yes, you are," Jess and Ashley said in unison.

"There. You girls are all set," one of the makeup artists said.

We all hurried toward the tall mirrors placed at the other side of the room. It might sound arrogant, but I was more than pleased with what I saw. My nails looked stunning, and the makeup had completely accentuated my best features. I looked like a movie star, and so did the others.

"This is awesome," I said, twirling around.

"Right? Now we'll look all amazing for our next activity," Ashley said. "Are you guys ready?"

"We are," Olive said. Her hair was curled and pinned up in a stylish manner.

"Could you snap a picture for me?" Suzie asked me. "I want to send this to Alex. God knows when I'll look this good again."

"Nonsense, you always look stunning," I said.

I snapped a couple of pictures and handed Suzie her phone back.

The seven of us gathered our handbags while Ashley settled the bill and Layla flung the inflatable toy around her body again. Ashley's orders.

The limo ride only took twenty minutes this time. The vehicle dropped us off at what looked like a shady warehouse, but when we got inside it turned out to be a trendy bar with six adjoining indoor laser tag rooms. The place was packed full of people. Loud music and the smell of beer drifted toward us. The floor was sticky from too many spilled beverages.

I looked at Jess for signs of her bolting again. She looked a bit pale.

"It's going to be fine," I told her.

"Let's hope I don't need to use the bathroom," she said.

Once we were all inside, Ashley led us to a table. "We're a little early and we'll have to wait for our opposition, so let's get some drinks first."

"I'm heading to the bathroom," I told Suzie. "That cucumber water passed right through me."

"Do you want me to order you something?" she asked.

I shook my head. "That's okay, I'll pass by the bar on my way back."

The bathroom contained more neon lighting and a rather long queue. I rummaged around in my purse until I found a packet of Skittles and cracked it open while the queue slowly progressed. Hours had passed since we left Old Pine Cove and we still hadn't eaten. And now we were about to go in for a game of laser tag, which would be exhausting for sure. I'd rather be prepared.

Fifteen minutes later, I could finally empty my bladder. On my way back to the group, I stopped by the bar to get myself a glass of sparkling water. I didn't want to drink any alcohol without having eaten a meal or I'd end up injuring myself during the game.

I put in my order with the bartender and slid onto a bar stool to wait for my drink.

"You seem to be an expert on this topic," a guy next to me said.

"I'm sorry, what topic would that be? Sparkling water?" I didn't understand what he was hinting at.

He grinned. "At being sexy."

Oh my word, seriously? Maybe that makeover hadn't been a great idea after all if it meant attracting weirdos.

"Uh, thanks, I guess," I said.

I zoned in on the bartender and tried to signal him to get a move on already, but I couldn't catch his eye. How long could it take to pour a glass of water?

"I'm Tony," the guy said.

Taking a hint didn't seem to be part of *his* expertise. Too bad.

"Okay," I said.

"And you are?"

I sighed. "Not really that interested. I'm here with a group, sorry."

He rolled his eyes. "So? I'm here with a group too. They don't mind me hooking up."

If my water arrived now, I'd chuck it in his face.

"I don't want to hook up, sorry," I said without looking at him.

I shouldn't have been the one to keep apologizing to Tony, but I didn't want to be completely rude.

"You say that now, but wait until you see this."

Okay, he had me there. I turned his way, half expecting him to pull a rabbit out of a hat, but instead he rolled up his shirt sleeve and flexed his bicep. I didn't know whether to laugh or cry.

"Good for you, but it's still a no," I said.

He bobbed his head up and down. "Okay, so you like to play hard to get. I can dig that."

"I'm not playing anything."

My words had barely left my lips when someone placed a hand on my shoulder and a low, familiar voice hit my ears. "Is this guy bothering you?"

My brain went into overdrive. Did Justin Miller just crash Layla's bachelorette party and swoop in to save me from Lonely Tony?

"How did you get here?" I asked, turning around.

"By car."

The guy made me roll my eyes so much that I might end up with permanent damage if he kept this up. "I mean, what are you doing *here*? This is Layla's bachelorette party, as in, no men."

He motioned with his head to a group of guys sitting

at a nearby table. "Ashley thought it would be cool to have Asher's bachelor party coincide with Layla's. We're going to beat you girls at laser tag."

"Beat us? You mean get beaten," I said.

Tony didn't like our chitchat at all, because he pounded a fist on the bar. "Excuse me, I was talking to this woman over here. Go find your own girl."

"Dude, she doesn't want to talk to you," Justin said, putting a protective arm around my shoulder. I didn't feel the urge to swat it away. In fact, it felt oddly nice to be in such close proximity to him once again.

"What are you, her boyfriend?" Tony asked with narrowed eyes.

Justin puffed out his chest. "Who cares who or what I am? If a woman says no, she means no."

"He's right," I said. "I did mean it when I told you no."

"Listen, missy—" Tony started, but the bartender cut our unpleasant conversation off.

"If you're here to look for trouble, think twice, pal. Either behave or get the hell out of this bar."

Tony muttered some curse words under his breath and walked away with stamping feet. I let out a relieved sigh. Good riddance, Tony.

I turned to Justin. "Thanks for helping me out, even though I didn't need saving."

He leaned against the bar. "You secretly love it that I save you from the big bad world."

"I don't. I can fend for myself."

"You can, but you love being saved by me. Just admit

it."

"Shut it, Jussie," I said with a laugh.

"You using that ridiculous nickname only spurs me on." He ran a hand through his hair. "You look amazing, by the way. I mean, you always look great, but today… Wow."

"Thanks," I said, grinning.

I thought back to the night he tried to sing me a song and I ran away like a fool.

"Justin," I started. "About the other night… I know we never talked about it, but I want you to know I only ran away because I was scared."

Right at that moment, the bartender put my glass of water in front of me.

Justin gave me a warm smile. "And you think I'm not scared to death? Look at you. You're this stunning woman, and I'm the guy who still gets looked at as the class clown. I don't know how I can ever live up to your expectations."

I swallowed. He thought he couldn't live up to my expectations? In my mind, it was exactly the other way around. How could I ever live up to his?

"I should go and join the rest of our group," I said, not knowing what to reply to his honest comment. I knew it was lame not to say anything more profound, but we only had a couple of minutes left before the start of the game and that wasn't nearly enough time to tell him how I felt about him.

"Okay then. I'll see you in there in ten minutes," Justin said, pointing at the laser tag rooms.

I hopped off the bar stool and grinned. "Get ready to

have your ass kicked by a group of girls."

He grinned, showing off his dimples again. "I can't wait."

I walked back to our table with a spring in my step. As soon as I slid into my chair, Ashley grabbed my arm. "What did he say?"

"What did who say?" I asked, sipping my water.

I knew all too well who she meant, but hoped I was wrong.

"Justin Miller, that's who. Did you tell him about me?"

"I didn't, sorry. I was too busy scaring off this annoying guy trying to hit on me."

Ashley let her gaze travel around the bar. "Who?"

I shushed her. "Don't. He'll notice and take it as a sign to come over here. Trust me, you don't want this guy to make an appearance at our table. Watching him flex his bicep once was more than enough."

Before she could start arguing with me or pressing the issue about introducing her to Justin any further, our group got called to laser tag room three.

"Aren't you happy we got a makeover, though?" Ashley said. "I knew the guys would be here and figured we might as well look stunning."

"Yeah, thanks," I said.

Was I the only one who thought it was weird to get a makeover to play a game in a dark room? Maybe all the pampering had been a ploy for Ashley to get her hands on Justin.

A fearful grip tightened around my heart. There was no

denying Ashley looked way prettier than I did. Justin would probably notice as well.

I glanced over my shoulder. Asher, Justin, and their friends got up, ready to follow us in there. My heart fluttered and I forced myself to take three deep breaths. I needed to get a grip. We were here to play an innocent game of laser tag, nothing more.

A staff member handed us all a special vest with sensors and a laser gun. Jess wiped hers down with a big blob of hand sanitizer before touching it. At least she didn't chicken out this time. I had to applaud her for her bravery.

"The girls here will be team green, the guys team red," the staff member announced. "Make sure to aim for the opposing party."

The guys were acting like typical guys at a bachelor party, each one louder than the next. They held their blasters toward one another as if they were having a light saber fight. Ugh.

Justin kept extremely quiet, though. I glanced at him when I thought he wasn't looking, but our eyes met each and every time.

I didn't listen to the rules the staff member rattled off in a boring voice, as my attention got swallowed up by Justin's appearance. The vest and laser gun made him look tougher than usual, especially with his feet planted firmly on the ground as if he was ready for a fight. His clean-shaven jaw shimmered in the neon lights. It was probably as soft as a pair of silk sheets. I felt the urge to run my hand over his smooth skin. Not just his jaw, but… everywhere.

I wondered if he knew we would end up in here together and decided to look particularly gorgeous.

The doors to the laser arena opened, excitement filling the air.

"Lock and load," Asher shouted, eliciting cheers from the other guys.

"I hope we survive this," Olive said.

She looked a bit shaken, but I assured her this was going to be fun.

"Remember, no running or climbing the obstacles," the staff member yelled at us, but no one paid attention to him.

Justin pushed past me. "See you on the other side. There's no escaping me in there."

The doors closed behind us and I held my laser gun pointed forward. Enough being sweet little Addy. It was time to hunt Justin down and maybe give Ashley a subtle push while I was at it. She'd never know it was intentional.

CHAPTER EIGHTEEN

My eyes needed a couple of seconds to adjust to the dark of the laser tag arena. Everyone around me scurried away, hiding behind wooden screens and inside small tunnels. I stepped right into a big net and let out a scream. A moment later, I got hit by a laser.

I stumbled out of the net and lowered myself behind the hood of a car. The arena must've been huge, considering the number of props that were stuffed in there.

I let my gaze travel around the room. A couple of feet in front of me was a metal staircase leading to the top level. I caught sight of a pair of red blinking lights, aimed my laser at them, and shot. Ha. Us girls could definitely win this.

Still crouched low, I made my way to another hiding spot. Ashley was taking cover there as well. "Psst," she said. "Listen, if you locate Justin, will you please introduce me?"

"Like, now? In the middle of a game?" I had to give it to her, she wasn't a quitter.

She shrugged. "Now's as good a time as any. I mean, I need to get to him before some other chick does."

"Maybe later. I'm trying to win this game," I said. "Oh look, someone's motioning for me. Gotta go."

I left our hiding spot and made a run for the stairs. I got attacked from behind, but the person pointing his laser gun at me missed all his shots. When I was in the clear again, I located Ashley and aimed at her, which wasn't hard to do since she was strolling toward the back corner of the arena as if she didn't mind being so exposed.

I ducked down as soon as I hit her with my laser. It was lame, but she was being lame too. Okay, maybe she was only trying to get what tickled her fancy, and I couldn't blame her for trying. That didn't mean I couldn't prevent her little plan from succeeding, though.

I moved through the arena in true Katniss Everdeen style and managed to nail at least fifteen shots. Justin's dark hair popped up from behind obstacles now and again, but he never stood still long enough for me to take him out.

Time flew by and before I knew it, we were called back to the vesting room for a five-minute break. Sweat dripped down my back. Who knew a game of laser tag would be this exhausting?

"Some idiot from our team shot me," Ashley said, clearly exasperated.

She stared everyone in our group down with a furious look in her eyes.

"Relax, it's just a game, Ash," Jess said, still panting from our twenty minutes of gameplay.

"Games need to be played fair," Ashley countered.

"I'm sure it wasn't on purpose," I said. "We're all trying to get used to handling these laser guns. The next round won't have these kinds of hiccups."

Ashley leaned against the wall, inspecting her blaster as if she was a soldier at war. "It better not. I don't want the guys to win this game."

"Three minutes," a computerized voice announced over the loudspeakers.

Olive appeared by my side. "This is all a bit too intense for me. The bickering, I mean. I'm loving the laser tag."

"I agree," I said, keeping my voice down. "Layla's friends sure are an fiery bunch."

"Right? And why does Ashley feel the need to flirt at her friend's bachelorette party? This day should be all about Layla. She could at least wait until everyone's out drunk or something."

I followed Olive's gaze and spotted Justin and Ashley talking in a corner of the room. She was touching his arm more than necessary and every time I saw his lips move, she threw her head back and laughed. Seeing her little act would make you think Justin was a renowned stand-up comedian. Sure, he was amusing, but he wasn't *that* funny. I should've just tackled her in there when I had the chance.

And Justin wasn't being fair either. A few days ago, he was performing a song for me and now he was flirting with another woman? I felt stupid for ever bothering with him.

The computerized voice counted backward from ten to zero and the doors to the arena flung open again. I stormed in, ready to take both Ashley and Justin down. I needed to funnel my energy into winning this game instead of fighting back the tears gathering in my eyes.

I took cover in the cockpit of a fake spacecraft. I hoped the plexiglass at the front was smudged enough so the others wouldn't notice me immediately. There was a convenient small hole at the side to take out anyone entering my perimeter.

A couple of minutes later, Justin crept closer. He sat right in my line of vision, but he hadn't spotted me as his back was toward me. This was my chance. I knew that he wouldn't care or be affected by my move in any way, but it sure would make me feel better.

I pointed my laser at his shoulder and pulled the trigger.

"Gotcha," I said, perhaps a tad too loud.

Justin turned around, eyes narrowed, blaster gun pointed in front of him. I ducked down, my heart racing. I hoped he hadn't seen me and would back off. But instead of running away, he approached my hideout.

Uh-oh. There was no escaping the cockpit. He'd catch me in here and take a shot at me for sure.

His footsteps banged on the metal and he peeked his head inside of my hiding place. I pointed my laser at him as a warning. "Don't come any closer."

"Did you just shoot me from behind?" he asked, taking a step closer. I guess my warning didn't impress him one bit.

"Maybe. Did you just flirt with the big-breasted friend of your best friend's fiancée?"

I slapped a hand over my mouth. Those were not the words I'd planned on uttering, especially not in that venomous tone.

Justin crouched down beside me. "Did I just do what now?"

"This place is too small to contain two people in a comfortable way," I said, completely ignoring his question in the hopes of him forgetting about it.

Of course, that lame tactic didn't fly with him.

"Why would me flirting with Ashley bother you?"

"So you know her name and everything," I said. "Priceless."

"Well, I'm not stupid. I am capable of remembering someone's name. I would hardly call that *priceless*," he said, using air quotes and everything.

I sighed. He was being impossible. "I'm sorry about bringing it up and about shooting you. Would you please leave now? Maybe Ashley has a hiding spot you can crawl into."

"I don't want to. I don't care about that girl, big breasts or not."

My eyes darted around the room, trying to avoid his. "You being here is making me feel all weird."

"Weird how?"

I rolled my eyes. "I don't know. On edge. Uncomfortable. Who wouldn't feel weird when they have to involuntarily spend time in an enclosed space with their nemesis?"

Justin put his blaster gun down. Then he sat so close next to me that I thought about giving him a spiel about personal space and how he had crossed the line of what was considered polite. But my breath caught in my throat when he settled those stunning eyes of his on my face, and I was rendered immobile.

"I'm not your nemesis. You want to think I am so you have an excuse for not kissing me."

All the air got sucked out of me. "Excuse me, did you just say kissing you?"

He laughed. "Don't look so shocked."

"I don't want to kiss you at all," I said weakly. Even I wasn't convinced.

He held his hands up in surrender. "Fine, then I'll go."

"No, wait." I grabbed his arm. "Please don't go."

He put his fingers on his temples as if it was all getting too much for him. "I told you at the party, Addy, and I'm going to say it one last time. I'm done playing games. Either you want me, or you don't."

I swallowed. "Nothing about this makes sense."

"It does to me."

I thought for a beat before speaking. "You used to think I was a silly girl, remember? That's why you made jokes at my expense, spread that stupid nickname around and ruined my science project. Why would you want me after all these years, huh? Why do you even care?"

"Forget about that stupid science project already. Did it ever occur to you that I was a dick to you in high school because I had a crush on you and I didn't know how to go about it? Besides, I never once called you a silly girl. That all happened in your imagination."

My eyebrows shot up, and a mix of confusion and elation scrambled my brains into mush. His comment reminded me of that evening at Roger's, when he told me he had his eye on me in high school. So, he was saying he used to make my life miserable because he *liked* me?

"Has anyone ever told you you talk with your face?" he asked.

"Oh yeah? What is my face telling you?"

He put a finger on my lips and it felt as if they were being licked by burning flames. "Shhh. Enough with the endless talking. I know you want me to kiss you. If you don't, you'll have to stop me. If you stay quiet, I'll take that as proof that you want me just as much as I want you."

He let his finger slide to the corner of my mouth and pulled my bottom lip down, stroking it left to right. Then he put his palm on my cheek. He looked at me as if I was a yummy treat he just needed to have.

My breath came out in shorter, louder pants. Justin licked his lips and leaned in, his nose barely touching mine. Wow. He sure liked to take his time.

My arms hung limp against my body. I couldn't move. I couldn't talk. All I could do was think about how I was about to kiss this gorgeous guy in the cockpit of a fake spacecraft, wearing a vest with blinking lights on it. If my heart wasn't racing, that thought would've undoubtedly made me crack up laughing.

Our mouths were only millimeters apart and I closed my eyes. His lips crashed into mine. I let out a moan. All the feelings I had locked away for so long exploded inside of me. Now that his hungry mouth had found mine, I couldn't deny it any longer. I wanted to kiss Justin more than anything.

I put my shaking hands on the nape of his neck and let my fingers run through his hair. Now it was him who was letting out a low moan.

He let his tongue run against mine and bit my lip, slowly tugging it. Fire shot to every nerve ending in my body. His hands were on my face, my neck, my back.

"Are you trying to kill me?" I said in between breaths.

"You're one to talk." His words came out all hoarse and urgent, just like his kisses.

The automated voice sounded over the loudspeakers again, announcing one more minute of gameplay. We both came up for air and locked eyes.

"You're going to be the death of me, Addison Grant."

I grinned. "The same goes for you, Justin Miller."

We found each other's mouths again and kissed like I'd never been kissed in my entire life. Then the lights came on, and the chattering voices of our friends drifted inside the cockpit.

"What if they see us together?" I whispered, my fingers intertwined with his.

"I'll go first."

I peered outside of the plexiglass. "Okay. I'm right behind you."

He grabbed his blaster gun and crawled out of our little love cave. I raked my fingers through my hair, hoping it looked semi-okay. I didn't want to raise any suspicion.

I picked up my gun and walked out of the arena as if I hadn't just experienced the most mind-blowing make-out session ever.

CHAPTER NINETEEN

How does one act normal and composed when one of the hottest, most popular movie stars of the year just kissed you and made you moan with pleasure? Exactly. It can't be done.

When Ashley excitedly announced that we would have dinner with the boys before parting ways again, I felt more anxious than Jess during that mud bath. There was no way I'd be able to eat and make conversation with Justin right there. I made a deal with myself to sit at the opposite end of the table so I could avoid him altogether. We could always catch up later, after everyone had gone home and we could be alone.

We headed to a Mexican restaurant a block from the laser warehouse. Ashley had conveniently positioned herself so that she'd be walking next to Justin. We were barely out of the door when she was laughing and touching him again. Only this time, it didn't bother me like it had before, because it was my lips he'd kissed, not hers.

"How are you doing?" Suzie asked, catching up with me. "It seems like we've hardly had any time to properly talk today."

"Everything is a-okay. No calls from the inn, no frantic Diane trying to get me to set up a table to sell vacuum cleaners at the wedding, no escaping ducks, and no unsatisfied customers. So, yeah, it's all gooood."

She narrowed her eyes. "Is something up? You're all sweaty and starry-eyed."

"It was intense in there. I did a lot of running, hence the red face. I'll be feeling it tomorrow for sure," I said. Then I stretched my arms above my head for good measure.

Suzie didn't look entirely convinced by my rendition of McSporty Girl, but didn't press the issue.

"Too bad we couldn't take a shower at that place." She pulled her t-shirt to air it out. "I'm all sweaty. It's a good thing we won, though."

"We did?" I asked.

"Addy, you can't keep fooling me. You didn't realize we'd won? Something is definitely up."

I shrugged. I didn't want to tell her about my sizzling kiss. Not before I'd had time to process it or before I talked to Justin. What if it was a one-off thing for him? I fiercely hoped it wasn't, though. I craved more of the same.

"It's nothing to worry about," I said. "I'm just feeling a

bit light-headed from barely eating all day."

"Oh, okay. Good thing we'll be eating soon, then. I'm starving as well, to be honest."

We all stepped inside of the restaurant and a waiter led us to a long table with eight chairs on either side. I managed to sit down at the far end, with Justin having to take a seat at the other side of the table. Good. At least with this distance between us, I'd be able to eat and avoid being a nervous stress ball.

Or so I thought. Ashley had to ruin my little plan.

"Excuse me, would it be possible to sit outside?" she asked the waiter.

"Of course, not a problem at all," he said.

We all got up again, the sound of chairs scraping across the floor filling the air. Layla's inflatable toy poked a waiter in the eye, and Jess dropped a blotch of hand sanitizer on the floor, but apart from that, no major dramas unfolded.

The outside area was decked out with wooden tables, colorful lanterns, and benches that sported cute throw pillows. The atmosphere was way cozier out there.

I once again managed to grab a seat at the far end of the table. Ashley plopped down next to me and waved to Justin, who was about to go sit at the other end of the table. "Here, I've saved you a spot. No need to go sit all the way over there."

He hesitated for a moment, his eyes darting toward mine. As soon as they met, I felt warmth creep into my cheeks, and I turned my head away.

"Addy and I don't bite, you know," Ashley said. She followed the words with one of her over-the-top *hahaha, I'm so funny* laughs.

Brianna was about to sit down opposite me, but Ashley threw her a fake smile. "I'm so sorry, but that seat's taken. Isn't that right, Justin?"

"Sure. Yeah, it seems like that's where I'm going to sit," he said.

I didn't like it one bit, but he was right to take Ashley up on her offer. Otherwise it would've raised suspicion, and the last thing I wanted was him to draw attention to us. What single guy wouldn't want to sit across from a beautiful girl like Ashley during a friendly dinner?

Brianna scooted over and Justin sat down next to her. This was just great. Not only was he right across from me, his knees touched mine under the table. Why did he have to be so tall? Normal-sized would've worked better in this predicament.

I blocked the view I had of Justin's perfect face with my menu and read it as if it was a critically acclaimed masterpiece. Never had I studied the description of fajitas so closely.

"Tell me, Justin, what's going on in your life?" Ashley asked, her voice syrupy sweet. "I hear you're still single?"

From behind my menu, I heard him cough. "Kind of."

"Kind of?" Ashley asked, her brows furrowed. "Shouldn't you know whether or not you have a girlfriend?"

My heart picked up speed. I wasn't Justin's girlfriend. All we had done was share a heavenly kiss, but we hadn't discussed what it all meant. I lowered my menu to peek at him.

"Let's say I'm single, but interested in someone," he said, not able to contain a smile.

I looked away and scanned the menu options. Would you look at that. The fajitas came with a serving of homemade, award-winning guacamole. Oh wow, and extra servings of sour cream could be requested for only a dollar more.

"Really?" Ashley asked, her eyes sparkling. "So am I. What a coincidence."

Did she assume Justin was talking about her? I lowered my menu to right below my eyes.

"You know," Ashley started, "if you are interested in this girl, I'm sure she would say yes if you asked her out."

Oh, puh-lease. Way to be subtle, Ash.

"I've asked her out already," Justin said. "It ended with her hiding in a pantry."

Brianna leaned in, eager to get the latest dirt on his love life. "That sounds intense. Is she in the acting business too?"

Justin pinned me down with a look while answering. "You could say that. She keeps saying she hates me, but tell me, would you girls kiss a guy you hated?"

What words were these? And when was that waiter arriving to take our order?

Brianna scrunched up her nose in disgust. "There's this one guy at work I can't stand. I don't even want to sit next to him during lunch time, let alone have him touch my mouth."

Justin nodded. "My thoughts exactly. And yet this girl kissed me in the most mind-blowing way."

I hid back behind my menu.

"Having trouble deciding, Addy?" Justin asked.

"Maybe."

Next to me, Ashley shifted in her seat, her expression full of shock. Then she elbowed me in the side and joined me behind the safety of the laminated menu pages.

"You could've told me he's involved with someone," she said with a hiss.

"I didn't know until today," I said, keeping my voice low. "Trust me, this is all brand-new information to me. I'm still processing it myself."

Ashley crossed her arms over her chest. She had the same expression a kid has when he doesn't get the toy he asked for.

"Well, I'm sorry for whoever this girl is, but I'm not stopping until I get what I want."

The determined look on her face made me cringe in my seat.

The waiter appeared at our table again to take our order. I went for the fajitas with the award-winning guac and an extra portion of sour cream.

"I'll have the same as her," Justin said as I put my menu down.

"Why?" I asked.

He exhaled patiently. "Why not?"

Brianna waggled her finger between us. "You two are acting weird."

"Justin always acts weird," I said. "It's his default behavior."

A foot touched my shin, and I jumped in my seat. This resulted in quite a few confused stares. "Sorry. There was something on my leg."

Justin snickered. I rolled my eyes at him, but inside I was rocking out to an upbeat song. He liked *me*. It was *my* leg he'd just touched under the table.

Our drinks arrived and Justin put his fork to his glass. Fifteen heads perked up, several people getting their phone out to film whatever he was going to say.

"I'd like to make a toast," he started. "I've known Asher my entire life and he's become like a brother to me. We grew up in Old Pine Cove together, where we had the best adventures. I'm so happy to see him with Layla. You two are such a beautiful couple."

An echo of *aww* went through the group.

"I also want to use this moment as an opportunity to apologize."

Layla's face went ashen. "What did you do?"

Justin laughed. "I didn't do anything to you two. This apology concerns Addy. She told me she would accompany me to Asher and Layla's wedding under the condition that I publicly apologized to her."

"Really?" Ashley said, giving me the stink eye. "He's taking *you* to the wedding?"

"That depends on this speech," I said.

Ugh. Did she really have to make it sound like it was unbelievable he would ask me to be his date to the wedding?

"Addy," Justin said, his full attention now on me. "I treated you in several not-so-nice ways back in high school. I ruined your science project. I came up with that horrible nickname. I laughed at you when you tripped in the cafeteria. I put that fake Valentine's card in your locker—"

"That was you?"

For years I had thought I had a mystery admirer. What an anticlimax to find out it was another one of Justin's antics.

"It was, and I'm sorry. I admit there are better ways to get a girl's attention. Believe me when I say that I was trying to get you to like me. Weird way of going about it, I know. I was a jerk and I truly feel sorry about all of it. I hope you can forgive me so that I can take you to the wedding."

I swallowed. "Yes, I do. Accept the apology, I mean. I don't mean I do as in I want to marry you."

Shut up, Addy. Please.

The entire group laughed and clinked their glasses together while I froze in my seat. Why did I talk about marrying the guy?

"Isn't that girl you kissed going to be pissed when she finds out that you're taking another girl to a wedding?" Ashley asked.

Justin sat down again and took a long swig of his beer. The tension was killing me. He'd better have a convincing, fake explanation, because I didn't want the truth to be out there already.

"I doubt she'll be mad," he said.

Good. Our secret was safe. For the time being anyway.

Ashley and Brianna exchanged a look. Brianna mouthed "*player*" and Ashley shrugged as if she didn't even care. The girl had no morals. Well, she was not going to get her hands on Justin. Not if I had a say in it.

I excused myself to go to the bathroom. When I was mid-pee, Justin's whispered voice reached me through the toilet doors. "Addy, you in there?"

"Just a minute," I said.

I wondered why he had followed me in there. I finished as fast as humanly possible, washed my hands, and rearranged my hair. Justin was standing just outside the bathroom entrance, looking as if he could get busted any minute. For what, I had no idea. Standing near a restaurant bathroom entrance wasn't exactly cause for calling the police on someone.

He leaned in, his lips brushing against my ear. The hairs on my neck shot up despite the fact that it was anything but cold in there. "We can't talk here, but meet me tomorrow at noon at the inn's parking lot."

I laughed so hard I needed to put my hand in front of my mouth to temper the sound. "Meet you tomorrow at noon? Are you planning to do a drug deal with me?"

He grinned. "Since kissing you makes me high, you could say I am indeed planning a drug deal."

"Shut up," I said and slapped his chest. It was awfully firm. "What if someone hears you?"

"Who would hear us out here? I checked the perimeter seconds ago."

I motioned in the direction of the restaurant. "People

having dinner. Our friends. A handful of crazy fans of yours who have tracked you down."

"Tomorrow. Noon. Don't be late," he said, skillfully ignoring my concerns. Then he disappeared into the men's bathroom.

I didn't have the faintest clue of what he had planned for noon the next day, but it would absolutely include kissing him again, and that was really all I needed to know.

CHAPTER TWENTY

Waiting for noon to roll around was excruciating. I had been up for hours and it was still only eleven, one hour until I could finally meet Justin.

The previous evening went down relatively well. I had to force myself to eat once the waiter brought our food to the table, because I was way too consumed with post-kiss feelings to have anything resembling an appetite.

Ashley didn't stop trying to lure Justin into her web all night. She wasn't even deterred one bit by the fact that Justin had admitted to kissing another girl. Thankfully, he kept skillfully turning the attention away from questions about his love life.

After dinner, we parted ways again. The guys went to

hit up a karaoke bar, and us girls went for cocktails at some fancy bar.

Once I got home and went to bed, I hardly slept because I couldn't get Justin out of my thoughts. I still couldn't believe he had kissed me. He had even posted that apology video online for the entire world to see. Every time I watched it, a bunch of butterflies did cartwheels in my stomach. Seriously, it was like an Olympic match in there.

Now I tried to stay busy with work, hoping that would make the time go faster. With the wedding only days away, another deposit had hit my bank account and I'd made an appointment at the bank to talk about a loan. That patch of land would finally be mine. So many exciting things were happening all at once that I constantly felt queasy. I didn't mind, though. After all, it was a good kind of queasy, not the I-ate-a-questionable-seafood-platter kind. Everything was coming together for me and I couldn't be more thrilled about several of my dreams becoming reality.

Diane walked into the lobby, heading straight to the reception desk. She'd come to do another inspection round – as she liked to call it – of the property now that the tables and chairs for the wedding dinner had been delivered.

"Everything okay?" I asked, flashing her my brightest smile.

"It looks good out there. We will have to go over the table setting again, though. Asher's Uncle Peter can't be sitting next to Aunt Vivian anymore."

I scribbled the info down on a Post-it. "I hope nothing bad happened?"

"If by bad you mean that Peter refused to buy a puppy and Viv reacted by kicking him to the curb, then yes," she said.

"Wow, okay. I'll make sure they won't share a table."

Throwing your husband out because of a puppy disagreement seemed like an awfully weird thing to do, but I didn't want to get into a discussion with Diane. After all, the shenanigans her family got up to were none of my business.

"Also, Layla told me one of her friends had requested to sit next to that Miller boy. There's nothing I can say about it – Layla is the bride after all – but I don't understand why anyone would make such a request. The poor girl must've been inhaling paint fumes."

I nodded. "Is this girl called Ashley by any chance?"

"That's right. She can have him, though."

Diane had only just finished speaking when Justin appeared at the top of the stairs. It was almost as if she'd summoned him by talking badly about him.

My hands started to shake as I wrote down the info. "I'll see what I can do," I told Diane, even though I didn't want to. But like Diane had stated earlier, it was Layla's wedding and she was the one who got to decide who sat next to whom.

Justin came to a standstill right behind Diane. Behind her back, he was miming the words she'd just uttered, making me snort.

Diane turned around and shook her head. "Speak of the devil."

Justin held his hands up, a smile tugging at the corners of his mouth. "I'm not looking for any trouble. Honestly, I don't know what I've ever done to you."

Diane's brows shot up. "May I remind you that you've dragged my Asher into questionable situations more than once? If and when you grow up, we can talk again."

Then she turned back to me. Her mouth transformed into a hard line. "I can count on you to make these changes?"

I tapped my pen on the block of Post-its. "Absolutely. It's all noted and will be taken care of."

"Good. See you soon, Addy." She walked toward the door, but as she grabbed the knob, she turned around. "Thank you for doing such a good job. I know it's been a stressful undertaking, but you've handled everything in a professional manner. Well, apart from that duck escaping, and having Justin around, but nobody is perfect."

As soon as the door shut behind her, Justin burst out laughing. "Why does a compliment from her sound like she's reprimanding you at the same time?"

"Beats me," I said, smiling at Justin like a certifiable fool.

"Are you free to go now?" he asked. "I know I'm early, but I couldn't wait."

I closed the computer's browser and logged off. "I am. Carter will arrive any minute. What did you have in mind?"

"Lunch? Somewhere quiet where we won't be disturbed."

"Sounds good. I have to be back in two hours, but everyone's got to eat, right?"

I grabbed my purse and joined Justin at the other side of the reception desk. We left the inn together. I had thought we'd go straight for his car, but instead he beckoned me to follow him on foot.

"Where are you taking me?" I asked.

"One of your favorite places in Old Pine Cove," he said.

"The bakery?"

He laughed. His hair fell in front of his eyes and I had to resist the urge to swipe it to the side.

"There," he said, motioning to the field in the distance. "You did want to buy this land, didn't you?"

"I do," I said.

He whistled out a breath. "Good. For a moment, I thought I'd made a mistake there."

"This is the spot," I said. "If everything goes according to plan, I'll have lots of animals here soon."

"You are going to get an alpaca, right?" he asked.

I shrugged. "Maybe. Didn't I tell you how expensive they are?"

"Well, never say never."

"I know. But I need to spend my money wisely. We can't all be millionaires like you," I said with a wink.

He put an arm around my shoulders and kissed the top of my head. "Who says I'm only a millionaire?"

My eyes grew wide. "You're a billionaire?"

He chuckled. "I'm just messing with you. Gosh, you can be fooled so easily."

"I'm having second thoughts about this outing," I said, making a fake angry face.

He grinned. "You so are not."

We found ourselves a small clearing near the edge of the field, surrounded by tall grass. No one would be able to see us here.

Justin put a blanket down, then started to unload his backpack. He placed two plastic flutes on a wooden tray. Then he pulled out a Tupperware container filled with strawberries, a couple of sandwiches wrapped in foil, and two bars of chocolate.

"Where did you get that?" I asked. "I don't recall Kermit the Frog lugging Tupperware around with him."

He laughed as he popped the lid off. "Mom gave it to me. I know, not exactly what you want to hear when you're on a date. But I did make the sandwiches myself. Extra mayonnaise and everything. I bet you Kermit the Frog himself couldn't make them taste as delicious, even if he wanted to."

"This is a real date?"

He cracked open a bottle of champagne and poured us both a glass. "I thought so, but we can call it anything you want to."

"Don't you think it's weird how the scale tipped from hate to… not hating each other?" I asked. I almost said *love*, but it was way too soon to think about that.

He put his drink down and handed me a sandwich. "For you, maybe, but I've always liked you. I just assumed the feeling was far from mutual."

We were both quiet while we munched on our sandwiches. Part of me wanted to put my arms around his waist and kiss him, but the other part of me was terrified. I wasn't looking to get my heart broken again.

"What's going on in that beautiful head of yours?" he asked, making the butterflies inside my stomach do somersaults again.

"I was trying to wrap my head around you and me. More specifically, our kiss yesterday."

His face lit up. "That was an unforgettable moment. Maybe we should do it again, though, to jog my memory of just how perfect it was."

He put his food down and I mirrored his move. My heart leapt into my throat as he wrapped his arms around my waist, exactly like I wanted to earlier.

I opened my mouth to speak, but his kiss ate my words before I could form them. His strong hands slid over the curve of my back. I let myself get lost in his kiss, savoring the magic of the moment with every fiber of my being.

He tasted like strawberries and champagne. I tugged on his hair and we came crashing down next to each other. Then I pulled away from his delicious lips. I didn't want to, but I needed to be smart.

"What's wrong?" he asked.

I let my shoulders drop and a heavy sigh escaped from my mouth. "I'm thrilled about what's going on between us."

"But?"

"I'm scared about where this will lead. If I give too much of myself to you, I'll be putting my heart on the line. I don't know if I'm willing to do that. Shouldn't we talk about all the ways getting involved with each other could hurt us?"

He leaned back on his elbows. "Or, we could talk about all the ways this would bring us joy and happiness."

"I want nothing more than for us to work out, but you're an actor, Justin. When would we ever see each other?"

He was silent for a moment. It didn't feel good to bring that up, but one of us had to before we took this any further. Before we crashed and burned.

"Yes, it's true that I love acting and sometimes I need to be in a certain place for an extended period of time. But that doesn't mean I'm locked away somewhere. We can still talk to each other." He turned sideways, his eyes nothing but honest. "I could go on a hiatus. There's this new movie they want me to audition for, but there will be other movies. There's only one you. I would hate to give up the chance to turn this into something more."

My heart set off a box of fireworks, but at the same time, a feeling of dread crept inside. "What if we don't work out and you've left your life behind for me? I can't let you do that, Justin. You'll start to resent me."

He shook his head. "I won't. I've been thinking about this even before I saw you again. It's part of the reason I came back to Old Pine Cove in the first place. Of course, I wanted to be here for Asher's wedding, but I also wanted some time to think about where to go next."

His words hit me right in the heart. He wasn't going anywhere soon, which meant that we would have time to work it out, to see where these feelings would lead us. And wow, did I wish they'd lead to him and me spending every minute together.

"You know, Addy," he started, "we could stop over-thinking everything and just enjoy each other's company while we're both here."

I grinned. "You mean kiss each other until we don't have any breath left?"

He pulled me toward him and smiled. "Yes, you sexy mind reader."

"Well, I can't say I'm opposed to that," I said and let my mouth land on his.

As far as I was concerned, we could keep doing this forever and I'd never grow bored of it.

CHAPTER TWENTY-ONE

I walked on clouds for the next forty-eight hours. Justin and I hadn't talked about the specifics of our relationship yet, but judging by the way he had kissed me between the Tupperware containers the other day, and again at my house the day after, he couldn't get enough of me. I felt the same way about him. Sometimes I couldn't wrap my head around how things had changed, but I'd decided to go with it and enjoy every minute of it.

And then he texted me about having a surprise for me. I didn't know what it was, but I was positive I'd love it. Heck, I'd be elated even if he gave me something small, like a fridge magnet or bottle opener. I couldn't believe how lucky I was.

We had agreed to meet for drinks after work. But first

I had an appointment with Sally at the bank. I crossed the town square to the building where my bank was housed. Since I had ten minutes to spare, I treated myself to a coffee at Sip'nBean and handed Olive a royal tip. Getting one step closer to acquiring the land I wanted made me happy, and I wanted to share that happiness with everyone I crossed paths with.

"This is truly generous of you, Addy," Olive said, tucking the money away in the tip jar on the counter.

I threw her a warm smile. "It's the least I can do. Things are going great. In fact, I'm about to push my career to a new level."

Her eyes lit up. "Me too! The tarot card readings for dogs aren't going too well, so I hired someone to make a professional flyer and I've already had three people set up an appointment with me today."

She shoved a stack of flyers in my direction.

"Tarot card readings for dogs," I read. "Get ten percent off with this flyer." I smiled at her. "These look great. Well done, Olive."

"You know, if you had a dog, I'd offer you a free reading."

"That's so nice of you. I'll keep that in mind should I ever adopt one."

"Great! Well, best of luck with your new business endeavor, Addy," Olive said, getting ready to serve another customer.

I waved her goodbye and made my way to the bank. I didn't have to wait long. Sally was punctual, a quality I admired in someone working with other people's money.

Her assistant led me down the hallway toward Sally's office. As soon as I was seated, she closed the door with a soft click.

"What can I do for you today, Addison?" she asked, sitting down with her hands resting on the desk in front of her.

"Remember how I was in here last year to talk about a business loan?" I asked. "Well, I finally have the required deposit."

Sally pushed her glasses toward the top of her nose. "Right. A loan to buy the Bensons' land. For a petting zoo, if I'm correct?"

I beamed. "Yes, that's right."

"Perfect," she said, opening a document on her computer. "Did you already put in an official offer with Mr. Benson?"

"Not really. I mean, he knows I'm willing to pay the asking price and I know that there aren't any other interested buyers."

She pushed her chair back to retrieve some papers from the printer. "Okay, what we could do right now is simulate the specifics of the loan. As soon as you've got a signed agreement with Mr. Benson, we can make it official."

"Great," I said. "Let's do that."

I answered all of Sally's questions, and gave her my accountant reports, cash flow statements, and other details she needed to know.

"Everything looks good on my side," she said. "You

have a great credit score and the fact that you can finance twenty-five percent of this acquisition with your own funds will definitely elevate your chances of approval. I think all that's left for you to do now is call Mr. Benson and tell him the news that you're ready to buy."

I wanted to jump up and hug her. This was fantastic news. "How long will it take for the loan to be approved?"

She tapped her chin with her finger. "I'd say three to six days after you've signed the papers with Mr. Benson."

"Thank you, Sally," I said. "I'll get right onto that."

When I left the bank, I couldn't stop smiling. I walked back to my car with a skip in my step and decided to drive straight to Mr. Benson's house to finalize the sale. We'd talked about me buying the land so many times, it was like a done deal.

I picked up a bottle of celebratory champagne on the way there and texted Justin that I had a surprise for *him*.

Gosh, I hoped Mr. Benson was home. Now that I finally had the finances to go through with this sale, I didn't want to wait a minute longer to make it official.

I rang the doorbell twice, but there was no answer. I decided to go around back, as he was probably working in his garden and couldn't hear the doorbell.

"Yoo-hoo, Mr. Benson," I called out while rounding the house.

I didn't want to scare him to death by suddenly appearing in his line of vision. I also didn't want to risk finding him sitting in his backyard with no clothes on. You could never be too careful with situations like these. When I was fourteen, I had accidentally witnessed my neighbor doing a naked dance with his garden hose. The image got imprinted into my memory forever, and him asking my mother to water his plants while he was on vacation never sounded the same again.

"Helloooo," I tried again.

I put a hand above my eyes to shield them from the sun. My shoulders fell. He wasn't here after all. Today wouldn't be the day.

But then he jumped out from behind a bush he was trimming, shears in his hands.

"Oh, hello, Addison."

"Mr. Benson, how are you?" I asked, barely able to contain my excitement.

He fiddled with his garden shears. "Yes, you know, I'm… uh… good."

My brows pinched together. What had he been doing behind that bush with those shears? I let my gaze wander to the blades, half expecting to see blood dripping from them.

"Am I catching you at a bad time?" I asked.

"Oh, no, it's not that," he said, waving the shears around in the air. I took a step back. "Why don't we have a drink and talk?"

"Sure, that sounds good," I said.

He put the sharp tool down and I let out a breath of relief. I knew deep down that he would never hurt me, but he was old, and what if he had Alzheimer's, thinking I was a trespasser he needed to attack with his shears?

I shook my head. I needed to get a grip. Mr. Benson was harmless, and only sixty-three. His mind was as clear as daylight on a summer's afternoon.

"How does lemonade sound?" he asked.

"Perfect."

I sat down in one of the wooden chairs on his back porch while he fetched us a pitcher of lemonade and some glasses.

He poured us both a glass and gave me a cautious smile. "I guess you're here to talk about the land?"

I nodded furiously. "I am."

His hand shook while he took a sip of lemonade. He got a handkerchief out of his pocket and dabbed his sweaty forehead.

"Are you nervous about parting ways with that patch of land?" I asked.

It couldn't be easy to leave behind something you've had your entire life. I knew for a fact that his parents had left the land to him when they died. And now it would become mine.

"Oh, that's okay, really. I'm getting too old to take proper care of it. It's just… I guess I'm relieved that you're taking it so well. I thought you'd be mad at me, even."

I put down my glass of lemonade. "Why would I be mad?"

"I knew you wanted to buy the land, but when that other offer came in—"

"Wait, what other offer?" I asked. I could feel the color leave my face. Maybe I misunderstood, and he'd said "brother cougher" or something. Not that *that* had any significant meaning, but it sure sounded better than "other offer."

"I sold the land yesterday, Addy. I'm sorry."

His words kicked the air out of my lungs. "But… how?"

"I should've asked you first, but I didn't know where you stood financially. I know we've been talking about me selling the land to you for ages, but you know… I needed the money. My wife's medical bills keep racking up and this person could pay me right away, plus ten percent extra."

This was unbelievable. While I had been out kissing Justin and frolicking around the inn, someone had bought the land I wanted, and crushed my dreams in one fell swoop.

Why? How? Who? Was it some hotshot who wanted to build a resort? A mall? This was terrible news. Not just for me, but for the entire town.

I tried to come up with a scenario that made sense, but I drew a blank. I couldn't even blame Mr. Benson for selling at such a great price, especially not when his wife was having expensive medical treatments. That didn't mean I didn't feel like crawling into a hole, though. I did my very best to fight off the tears that were desperate to break free.

"Are you okay?" Mr. Benson asked. "You haven't spoken in five minutes now."

"Who bought the land?"

He patted his forehead with his handkerchief again. "I'm afraid I can't disclose that information. But if it means anything, I do know that all will be revealed in good time and you most likely won't be opposed."

He was delusional. Why wouldn't I be opposed to someone hijacking my dream?

"Oh, look at the time," I said, glancing at the invisible watch around my arm. "They're expecting me at the inn. It's so late there's probably a search party out for me. I can't have them worry."

Mr. Benson walked me to my car, but I was too dazed and confused to hear a word he was saying. All I could think about was how the inn wouldn't be getting a petting zoo after all.

"Well, take care, Addison." Mr. Benson wrung his hands. He looked visibly shaken by the choice he'd made. Still, that didn't dull my disappointment.

"Good luck trimming your bush," I said before starting the engine.

He waved me off. As soon as I was out of sight, the tears I'd been holding back started streaming down my face. The day had started off on such a high note and now the dream I'd worked toward for years had come crashing down.

At least I still had Justin's company to look forward to. I was sure he'd be able to cheer me up, or at least help me to temporarily forget about losing something that had been mine in my heart, but never actually had been mine in real life, and now never would be.

CHAPTER TWENTY-TWO

By the time I stepped into Dave's Diner to meet Justin for dinner that night, I felt even worse. The cogs in my head had been turning nonstop the entire afternoon, despite the fact that I needed to stay focused with the wedding just around the corner. It turned out that overthinking didn't solve anything. All it had accomplished was wasting precious time and energy. Plus, mystery was best paired with cookies, so I had been eating treats nonstop and feeling nauseous.

It was hard realizing that I had to put a big red cross over my plans. If Mr. Benson had told me earlier that there was another offer, then I might've been able to match it. But the way he'd handled it meant I didn't stand a chance. There was nothing I could do now. The papers had been signed by this mystery buyer. It was over.

Justin waved me over to the booth at the far end of the diner where he was waiting for me. I slid into the seat across from him and gave him my best smile. I didn't want to put a damper on our date, so I tried to act as if nothing had happened. He reached over, cupped my face, and kissed me with such intensity that I was afraid I'd turn into a gooey puddle.

"I missed you," he said, even though we'd seen each other the evening before.

His words made me grin. "Me too."

Justin's phone rang, but he declined the call without even looking at the screen.

"Shouldn't you take that?" I asked. "It could be important."

He covered my hand with his and slowly stroked it with the tip of his thumb. "More important than spending time with you? I doubt that."

I opened my mouth to speak, but the chirping sound of his phone cut me off. Justin let it pass again, but when it rang for a third time, he couldn't ignore it any longer.

"I'll be right back," he said, letting out a heavy sigh. "Why don't you go ahead and order? I'll have a burger."

"Sure," I said.

I got out one of the menus shoved between the napkin holder and the condiments and scanned it. It was nothing more than a way to keep busy, though. I knew the menu choices at this place by heart and always ordered the same thing. The burgers at Dave's Diner were to die for.

Moments later, Leanne appeared. She took a pen and notepad out of her apron and shot me a welcoming smile. Leanne was a doll, or at least she was to me. She wasn't very fond of outsiders or tourists, but the townspeople all held a special place in her heart. "What can I get you, sweetie?"

"We'll both have the burger and fries. Oh, and could you bring a pitcher of water and a soda? I don't know what Justin wants to drink," I said.

"Sure thing." She let her gaze travel to the spot outside where Justin was talking on the phone. "Can you believe how much he's grown? I remember him and his friends being insufferable teenagers, and look at him now. Quite the catch."

I let my chin balance on my hands and sighed. "It's quite unbelievable, I'll tell you that."

"Well, I'll get Dave working on those burgers," Leanne said. "And take a napkin. I don't want you drooling all over my diner." She winked and stuffed her notepad back in her apron before returning to the kitchen.

I put the menu back and watched Justin through the window as he talked on the phone, trying to keep my saliva inside my mouth. His features had hardened, and his shoulders were slumped. He kept shaking his head. That phone call didn't look like a good one. I felt for him. There was nothing like that punch of bad news hitting you in the gut, especially when you least expected it. Whatever news he'd received, we could be miserable together.

When he walked back in, confusion was written all over his face.

"Are you okay?" I asked. "You look kind of pale."

He swallowed and put his phone on the table, then started rubbing his temples. "I… Er… That was my agent."

"Are they cancelling *In Dire Need*?" I asked.

He blew out a puff of air. "No."

"Then what's wrong?"

His eyes met mine and dread crept upon me. His expression clued me in on the fact that whatever news he had would affect me in a bad way.

"Actually, they offered me a part in a movie."

I furrowed my brows. "That's good news, right?"

"It is."

"Then why do you look like you've seen a ghost?"

He waited a beat before answering my question. "They want me to play the lead in the upcoming Crocodile Man remake."

My eyes grew wide. Crocodile Man was one of the world's most popular superheroes as well as a billion-dollar franchise. This would catapult his career faster than I could blink. "Wow, Justin, you're going to take it, right? This is the opportunity of a lifetime."

He shook his head. "I don't know. They have certain requirements. Giant ones. It's not like those movies where they ask you to shave your hair off or lose ten pounds."

"Then what do they want?" I asked. "I'm sure it can't be that bad."

He swallowed. "They want me to sign a contract that stipulates me not having a romantic relationship for at least a year. Apparently, the public prefers their superheroes to be single. It's good for profits and marketing," he said, his voice shaky.

"They can't do that, right? I mean, they can't interfere with your personal life like that."

Justin scoffed. "They can, believe me. It's their way or the highway."

I tried to meet his eyes, but he wouldn't let me. "So if you agree and take the role, we won't be able to see each other anymore?"

He coughed, then nodded. "Yes. I don't want to lose you, Addy. But this is Crocodile Man."

This is Crocodile Man. The words every girl dreams of hearing.

My arms felt like lead and my mouth hung slightly open. I couldn't find any words, or move. Justin was ditching me, before we had even truly begun developing this relationship, or whatever it was that we shared.

In my head, I tallied up my losses so far. There was the land that got snatched up right before I had the chance to buy it, and now Justin was telling me he was going to choose some superhero role instead of me. All I had to do now was wait for another disaster, as bad luck always came in threes, no?

"Here you go," Leanne said, and placed our burgers down. She had walked to our table without me even noticing. "Enjoy."

I stared at the burger and fries in front of me. My appetite had completely vanished.

"Addy?" Justin asked. "Aren't you going to say something?"

I shook my head. I had to bite my lip to keep myself from crying. "There's nothing to say."

"This doesn't have to mean the end for us, you know."

I shoved my plate away and put my elbows on the table so I had a place to rest my head. "A year without seeing each other? That *does* mean the end for us. I thought you told me you were thinking of taking a break from acting? What's changed between now and then?"

Justin leaned back in his seat and held his hands up. "I know, you're right. I did say that and I meant it at the time. But this is Crocodile Man. It's a huge opportunity."

Again with the Crocodile Man. I got it. Crocodile Man was every boy's dream, unlike me. I wasn't anyone's dream. Not anymore.

"Look," he continued. "I get that you don't understand what this means, but I can't say no to it."

"Why wouldn't I understand? Because I'm nothing more than a dumb small-town girl?"

He shot me a surprised look. "That's not what I said. Don't twist my words, Addy. Look, I don't like it either, but this is how Hollywood works."

Our realities had never seemed further apart. I had been delusional if I ever believed we stood a chance. He was a guy who flew helicopters and didn't flinch at an eleven-thousand-dollar suit. I drove an old car and bought my clothes off the rack during a sale. The gap between us was too big to cross. I hated for it to be true, but it was.

"So, this is it for us?" I asked, trying to keep the tears

from streaming down my face. I didn't want to make a scene at the diner. This punch in the gut called for a private crying session with copious amounts of Glen and Barry. Or the real deal. I had plenty of money now that I couldn't buy the land for my petting zoo. I might as well splurge on tubs of brand-name ice cream.

Justin shook his head. "It doesn't have to be. We could stay in touch. Have secret dates."

"I don't want to hide."

"I don't want to either, but I can't break my contract. They'd sue me without blinking."

"If you're taking this job, then fine. But you'll lose me."

His silence told me he'd already made his choice. I got up and threw a ten-dollar bill down for the food and drinks. "I think I should go."

"Please don't, Addy," he pleaded. "Stay and talk about this."

"There's nothing left to say," I said.

"Well, what about the wedding?"

I rolled my eyes. "The wedding? Seriously? Find someone else to be your plus one, because it isn't going to be me. I hear Ashley is still available and very eager."

I ran out of Dave's Diner without looking back and let the tears that were choking me run free. For a moment I'd hoped Justin would run after me, but as I got into my car, he was nowhere to be seen. It was all over.

I never thought I'd have to admit it, but Diane had been right after all. Justin Miller was trouble and it was sad that I'd only discovered it after putting my heart on the line.

CHAPTER TWENTY-THREE

The inn had never been busier. All kinds of people were scurrying around, trays of clean glasses were being put on tables, every spot was being dusted one last time. And I had taken refuge in the small room where we kept the cleaning supplies. I couldn't stay away for long, since Asher and Layla were getting married in a couple of hours, but I needed a five-minute breather.

Justin hadn't stopped calling me for an entire day. When he got the clue that I wasn't planning on answering, he had started sending me text messages. They ranged from apologies and pleas to talk to him, to gifs of Kermit the Frog looking out of the window, a sad look on his face.

No matter how much I wanted to feel his strong arms around me again, I couldn't let that happen. I didn't want to be with someone I could only have secret rendezvous with. If I committed to a relationship, it would have to be with a guy who was there for me, always. I mean, what if a year without us being together turned into two, then three? Crocodile Man was so popular that they'd probably make a gazillion sequels. It was a gamble I wasn't prepared to take.

There was a firm knock on the door. "Addy?"

I pushed the door ajar and Carter's face came into view. "I know you told me not to bother you for five minutes, but I need you outside. There's a problem with the length of the red carpet."

"I'll be right there," I said. "Thanks, Carter."

"Great, I'll tell Diane you're on your way."

I took three deep breaths, slapped on a smile, and marched outside. Diane was arguing with one of the guys from the party rental business we had hired. He looked seventeen, tops, and terrified.

"I hear there's a problem with the red carpet." I threw the guy a reassuring smile. "Maybe I could help."

"A problem? You mean a disaster. The red carpet is ten inches too short. Ten whole inches." Diane uttered the words with such volume that I cringed.

"I'm sure we can fix that, can't we?" I asked the teenager. By now he probably regretted taking on an after-school job.

"I'm going to get my boss," he said. "We might have an extra in the van."

He scurried away like a scared rabbit.

Diane's nostrils flared and I put a hand on her arm.

"Why don't you go inside and get yourself a drink? I'll ask Alex to make one especially for you."

She pushed my hand away and rubbed the spot as if I had put my germs all over her. "I can't. I'm needed out here."

I looked her in the eye. "Diane, listen to me. This is a stressful day for everyone involved, but weddings are all about love and joy. I wouldn't want you to get caught up in the details. You can trust me to take care of them. This day will be over before you know it and you'll never forgive yourself if you don't enjoy yourself."

She pursed her lips and pushed air out of her nose. "I guess you're right. Do you promise you have everything under control?"

I nodded and put my hand on her back to gently nudge her inside. "I do. I'll take care of the red carpet and then I'll go check on the bride. You've got nothing to worry about."

I approached the teenager, who was standing near the company van. "Excuse me. About the red carpet?"

The guy flinched, probably thinking I'd get mad at him as well.

"I just wanted to see whether you guys will be able to fix this. If not, I'm sure there's another solution," I said with a smile.

The guy's features relaxed. He called his boss over, who nodded and opened the doors to the van. "We have a spare one that we can use."

"Thank you," I said. "And sorry about before."

The boss let out a laugh. "Don't worry about it. The

kid got scared, but if he wants to work in this industry, he'll have to toughen up. I've had people freak out over the most insignificant things. Trust me, I've seen it all."

As soon as the red carpet was replaced with one ten inches longer, I went upstairs to check on the bridal party. Asher and Layla weren't going to spend their wedding night at the inn, but I had offered them two of our new floral-themed rooms to get themselves – and their bridesmaids and groomsmen – ready for the wedding.

Just as I rounded the corner of the top floor, Justin came out of the groom's room. He looked just as surprised as I was. Not that I was surprised to run into him here. He was still a guest at the inn, as well as the best man. But seeing him again for the first time since I ran out of Dave's Diner was shocking to say the least.

"Addy, can we talk?" he asked. "Please?"

Man, did he have to look this good? He was wearing one of the suits we'd bought the night of Claire's birthday party. He looked like a real gentleman. The suit accentuated his strong features like his broad shoulders and well-formed chest. His hair looked impeccable, and his jaw was freshly shaven. I knew how soft it would feel if I ran my hands over his face, but I couldn't. That ship had sailed and disappeared over the horizon.

Still, no matter how good he looked, his expression was horrible and reminded me a lot of how I felt. Defeated, disappointed, hurt, confused.

He had dark circles under his eyes as if he hadn't slept for days. They only made him look more ruggedly handsome, though.

"I don't have time," I said. "I have to check up on the bride and then I'm needed in the kitchen to see if we're still on schedule."

I thought I'd be able to stay cool and confident when running into Justin, but in reality, my voice sounded shaky, and my heart leapt into my throat.

He gave me a weak smile and slumped his shoulders. "Of course, I understand."

I mumbled a thank you and hurried away toward Layla's room, but Justin called my name again before I got there.

"Yes?" I asked without turning around. I couldn't deal with facing him right now. If I did, I'd burst into tears.

"Since you won't be my date to this wedding, Asher has arranged for Ashley to be my partner for the day. This doesn't change how I feel about you, though. Anyway, I wanted to let you know so you wouldn't get the wrong idea about me. I'm not interested in Ashley whatsoever."

I swallowed my tears down. "Thanks for letting me know."

Justin may have been speaking the truth about not being interested in her, but Ashley would stop at nothing to get Justin where she wanted him. Naked. In bed. With her. A shudder ran through me. I tried to cancel out any thoughts I had of the two of them hooking up and dashed into Layla's room.

"Addy," Brianna called out to me.

"Hey, guys," I said.

Jess jumped to her feet and sprayed some hand sanitizer

onto a glass of champagne, then shoved it into my hands. I politely declined. I had to work, and alcoholic beverages wouldn't help with getting to the end of this day unscathed.

"How are all you lovely bridesmaids doing?" I asked, looking around the room. "And what about you, Layla?"

"I'm doing fantastic, albeit nervous," Layla said. "I can hardly believe today is the day. Somebody pinch me."

Ashley turned around, a string of her long hair twisted around a curling iron. "Tell me about it. I get to walk down the aisle with Justin Miller today. Who knows? If I play my cards right, I might walk down the aisle to marry him someday."

I wished it wouldn't be considered unprofessional to throw something at her, preferably something hard like a hairbrush. Marry him? Good luck. As long as he was Crocodile Man, he wasn't marrying anyone.

"Well, do you girls need anything else?" I asked, silently hoping they didn't. Spending time with Ashley while she gushed about Justin being her date was far from what I needed.

"No, but why don't you stay for a while?" Stella asked.

I shook my head. "I can't. I'm needed in the kitchen."

Layla waved a hand at me. "Oh, come on, no one will know. If anyone asks, just tell them you were needed here to handle some crisis."

"I guess five minutes couldn't hurt," I said and took a seat on the bed.

The girls continued chatting. They talked about the lingerie Layla had bought and the guys they were hoping to dance with later.

I let my gaze wander around the room. Layla's dress hung from a velvet hanger, nothing more than the contours visible through the garment bag. Her white lingerie was on the dresser, the tags still on it.

She was one lucky girl, getting married to the man who loved her. The man who wouldn't blow her off in favor of some stupid superhero. I balled my hands into fists as I thought about Justin breaking the news about his job offer.

Marissa, the makeup artist, put her brush down and smiled. "There, all done."

She'd turned Layla into a gorgeous bride, and I felt my eyes water up. I dabbed them with a tissue, pretending there was something in my eye. If I already felt this emotional now, what kind of sobbing mess would the ceremony turn me into?

Marissa shot me a look. "Would you like me to do your makeup as well?"

"Oh, that's sweet, but I'm not one of the girls who booked your services."

She shrugged. "I'm paid by the hour and still have forty minutes left. Everyone else is ready, so why not? Come on, it'll make you feel better."

My eyebrows shot up. Did Justin tell them what had happened between us? I swallowed. "Make me feel better?"

Jess shot me a look. "I don't want to be rude, but Marissa is right. You look like a tragedy went down."

"Is everything okay?" Layla asked.

I plopped down in the chair in front of the desk where

Marissa's makeup and brushes were strewn around. "I guess hosting your wedding at the inn has made me nervous."

It was only half a lie. The wedding had brought me so much stress, you'd think I was the one tying the knot.

"I understand," Marissa said. "But just in case it's also boy trouble, let me help you look even more stunning than you do."

Did she have a sixth sense or something?

Marissa set to work and twenty minutes later, she was done. I took a look in the mirror and gasped. I had never looked this good before. Marissa had made my best features pop and I could've fooled myself into thinking I was a celebrity.

Eat that, Crocodile Man.

Brianna topped off everyone's champagne glasses and I quietly disappeared, but not before profusely thanking Marissa for making me look like a goddess.

I shut the door, leaving the chattering and clinking of champagne glasses behind me. As I descended the stairs, my phone started to blow up. I hoped it wasn't Diane with another ridiculous crisis that needed tending to asap.

I fished my phone out of my pocket and glanced at the screen. Huh. There were dozens of Instagram notifications, all from Justin's account. Apparently, he had been tagging me in posts and stories.

Without hesitating, I opened the app and looked at his content. All over his stories feature were short clips of him, telling his fans about how he had a surprise for a special person and how he was going to reveal it later today.

Huh. I had forgotten about his surprise. At least, I assumed this surprise he had told one and a half million people about was the same one he had texted me about a couple of days ago.

I put my phone away before I got flooded with hope. No matter what surprise Justin had in store for me, it wouldn't be enough to fix the actual problem. He was leaving me behind with nothing but the memory of a few dazzling kisses, to chase his dreams. It hurt like hell to realize I wasn't a part of that dream in any way.

CHAPTER TWENTY-FOUR

"And that's how Layla and I got the nickname The Wildflowers in college."

Ashley laughed and touched Justin's arm. *Again.*

The ceremony had been beautiful, and just as tear-inducing as I'd thought it would be. Asher and Layla both looked stunning, and made everyone cry when they said their vows. And they even had their dog, Peanut, be the ring-bearer.

But one hour into this dinner and I was ready to strangle Ashley. She had done nothing but gawk at Justin, telling him tons of wild stories about her college years, and touching him every chance she got. Which wasn't hard to do as they were seated next to each other.

I rolled my eyes and channeled my anger into my bread roll. I shredded the thing into six pieces, then royally buttered every single one of them.

Before dinner, I had tried to rearrange the table seating, but it was impossible to do without causing delays so I sucked it up and decided sharing a table with Justin wouldn't be *that* bad. Boy, had I been wrong.

Despite the fact that I was seated three chairs to the right of Justin, he constantly tried to get my attention with silly things like asking me to pass the salt or requesting the bottle of sparkling water to be sent his way.

He didn't look one bit impressed by Ashley's over-the-top stories and laughs, though. Good.

"That reminds me of Justin and me in college," Asher said. "Always pranking everyone. It was priceless."

I harrumphed. "Typical."

Justin's eyebrows shot up. "So you *do* speak."

I threw my butter knife down. "Excuse me?"

Everyone at the table fell silent. Layla's parents shifted in their seats.

"Well, you've refused to talk to me for days, and now all of a sudden you've got something to say about my college years?"

I shrugged. "I only said you pranking people sounds exactly like you."

He looked at me with a hurt expression on his face. "So you're back to hating me?"

I didn't answer. I secretly pined for him and felt horrible for how things had gone down between us, but that wasn't a detail he needed to know. In a couple of days, he'd be gone anyway.

"I promised you I'd prove you wrong and I still intend to do that," he said. "I'm not the immature jerk you make me out to be."

"Okay." I mumbled the words into my glass of water.

I hadn't meant for the atmosphere to get so awkward. Luckily Brianna got up and saved me from further awkwardness by giving a speech about the happy couple.

Meanwhile, Justin was throwing pleading looks at me. He kept gesturing to my phone, which I had placed next to my plate in case someone needed me. Technically, I had to be on call until the last guest left.

I looked at the screen and opened Justin's text message.

I'm going to prove you wrong. Just wait and see.

Then he got up and whispered something to Asher, who gave him a thumbs up, and left. What the heck did he have planned?

Before I could subtly ask Asher, Diane tapped me on the shoulder. "Do you have a moment?"

"Sure," I said and followed her to a spot out of earshot of the other guests.

"Addy," she started, a light slur to her words. Maybe telling her to drink something to calm her nerves hadn't been the best idea. "I feel like I should thank you for the hard work you've done. This wedding wouldn't have been possible without your dedication."

I smiled. "Thank you, Diane. I really appreciate you saying that."

"After the lovebirds have cut the cake, I will be announcing my special vacuum cleaner sale. It's a win-win, really. Guests get to attend a lovely wedding and they can go home with a brand new TurboVac5000 Diamond Series," she said, her eyes glistening as she spoke.

I chuckled. "Who doesn't love a win-win, am I right?"

She pressed one of her red fingernails into my chest and whispered, "I'm gifting you one, for free. As a thank you for your hard work."

"Aw, that's sweet."

Diane nodded. "So are you, Addy. You're one sweet cookie."

Wow. Those were the nicest words I'd ever heard Diane speak in my presence. I was about to do something crazy – hug her – when screams pierced the air.

I spun on my heel and spotted Duckota running between the tables. How on earth had she escaped? Her quacks sounded stressed, almost as if something was chasing her.

That's when I saw it. A baby alpaca came running toward us, knocking over chairs.

I gasped. Next to me, Diane had frozen in place. Her lip was trembling, and her hand had shot up into the air, but she was rendered mute.

Asher and Layla's dog started barking like crazy at the alpaca. Thank goodness Olive got to him before he could cause any damage. She gently pulled on his leash and led him away from the commotion.

"Wow, slow down, little fella," someone dressed like Kermit the Frog called out to the baby alpaca.

I snapped out of my shocked state and approached Duckota. I needed to save her before something happened to her. Scared people were known to do the weirdest things.

As soon as I had secured my duck, I zoomed in on the Kermit figure. He had the same build as Justin, the same hair, the same shoes… Okay, there was no mistake possible; it *was* Justin.

The baby alpaca hid itself under the bridal party's table, but Justin was able to lure the poor thing out with some bread rolls.

He picked the animal up and walked to the wooden dance floor. Then he spoke into the microphone, causing everyone to cringe because of the feedback.

"Sorry about that," he said, taking a step back.

By now, people had gotten their phones out and were filming every move he made.

"Sorry about the broken glass and everything. I'll make sure to fix this, but first I need to fix something else," he said. "Addy, would you please join me?"

I reluctantly made my way to the dance floor.

"Why are you dressed like Kermit the Frog?" I asked, half-laughing.

He grinned. "I thought it would be cool for the theme to be consistent."

"What theme?"

"All will be revealed shortly. But first you have to promise me you won't run away and go hide in a pantry."

I smiled. "Okay."

"Addy," he said, and I swear everyone held their breath for what was coming next. "These last couple of days have been extremely hard on me. When we shared that tantalizing kiss last week, I was over the moon. But then it all got taken away from me. All because of Crocodile Man."

"Yeah, well. Life's tough," I said, the painful memory making me tear up.

The baby alpaca in his arms tried to break free. One of Asher's cousins rushed toward us and took the animal from him.

Justin took a deep breath and grabbed both my hands. "That's true, but life without you is even tougher. I told my agent that I would only do this movie if they delete the clause about not dating anyone from the contract."

"And?" I asked, hope fluttering in my heart.

"And I'm not going to sit around and wait for their answer. I want to be with you, Addy. I'm head over heels for you."

"You are?"

He beamed at me and squeezed my hands. "I am, and I want to make your dreams come true."

"Why me, when you could have anyone?"

He laughed. "Oh, Addy, because you're you. You're nothing like those women chasing me for the money and the fame. I feel safe with you. And I want you to feel safe with me. I adore you. That's why I got you a surprise."

"Right, your mysterious surprise," I said. "The one you

posted about on Instagram?"

He nodded. "Last week, when I was at Sip'nBean, I overheard Mr. Benson talking about an offer he had gotten on the patch of land you wanted. I knew how much it meant to you, so I approached him afterward and made him an offer he couldn't refuse."

I gasped. "You did what now?"

He chuckled. "I bought the land for you, Addy. And this baby alpaca," he said, gesturing to the cute little animal, "is yours to keep as well. Consider it the first of many baby animals to come. I thought we could name the furry cutie Kermit. What do you think?"

Tears streamed down my face, most likely smudging my impeccable makeup, but I couldn't care less. Justin had made my dreams come true. All of them.

"Are you sure you want to know what I think?" I asked with a smile. Then I took the microphone from him and switched it off. This was something I needed to say to him without the message being broadcast to all of the wedding guests.

"Of course I do."

I put my arms around his neck and our noses touched. Justin let his hands rest on the small of my back, and let out a soft sigh.

"I think I love you, Justin. No, I don't think," I said, shaking my head. "I *know* I do. I love you as Kermit the Frog, as Crocodile Man, but first and foremost, I love you for being Justin Miller."

His mouth crashed into mine. I let out a small moan

and basked in the moment. His hands ran tenderly across my back, and I tugged on that gorgeous hair of his.

"Before we take this any further, there's one more thing I've got to do," he said, pulling back.

Asher rushed forward, handing him a guitar.

"You never gave me the chance to sing this song for you," Justin said.

"Aren't you going to steal Asher and Layla's thunder?" I asked.

"No one can steal my thunder today, lovely. Don't worry about it," Layla called out to me, putting her arm around her husband and beaming with joy.

Justin strummed his guitar. I couldn't stop the happy tears from falling down while he serenaded me with the most beautiful words anyone had ever spoken to me.

When the last notes had faded, I ran into his arms.

Around us people were murmuring in excited tones, and the DJ sent the starting notes of a love ballad into the ether. The dance floor filled up with other couples, but I only had eyes for my man.

Justin's mouth left mine, only for a moment, and he cupped my face with his hand. He let his thumb run over my lips, just like he'd done when we first kissed. "I love you too, Addy."

Then his mouth found mine again and I let myself get lost in his kiss, exploring every inch of him. Loving someone had never felt this good.

EPILOGUE

Two years later

"And you know Kermit has a vet's appointment next week, right?" I asked, feeling nervous about leaving my cute animals behind for ten days. Kermit had grown into a full-sized alpaca now, and I enjoyed cuddling him.

Carter put his hand on his hip. "Addy, relax. I'm going to take great care of Kermit, Duckota, and the rest of the furry gang. You shouldn't stress about veterinarian's appointments or feeding schedules. You're flying to L.A. for the Oscars, for crying out loud!"

I grinned. "I know, right? Do you think he'll get it?"

"Who will get what?" Justin's mesmerizing voice reached me, and I spun around.

"Hey, you," I said. I closed my eyes and we kissed, taking our sweet time. "You taste like cookies."

He laughed. "You keep baking them. What's a guy to do?"

"Carter and I were just talking about the Oscars. Personally, I think you're going to win."

Justin put his arm around my shoulder. "You're only saying that because it's your obligation to support me."

"My obligation?"

"Yeah, because you're my wife," he said.

I beamed at him. "I know, I just wanted to hear you say it again."

"What, wife?"

Carter rolled his eyes at us, but only in mock irritation. "You two are disgustingly cute, do you know that?"

"Yep," Justin said. "But I'm afraid we don't have a lot of time to talk about that. Our flight leaves in two hours and we still have to drive to the airport."

Carter pulled me into a hug. "Be safe and don't think about home, okay? The petting zoo's in good hands with me."

"Thanks, Carter."

We waved goodbye and walked toward my house – excuse me, our house – to get our suitcases and load them into the car.

"Ready?" Justin asked as he shut the trunk.

"I'm ready, Crocodile Man."

He opened the door of the car for me, but gently stopped me from getting in. Instead, he pulled me into a hug and put a kiss on the top of my head. Even after two years of bliss with him, I still had to pinch myself from time to time. His strong arms around me, his familiar scent, his mind-blowing kisses… I loved all of it. More importantly, I loved him.

He was still acting, but only took on movie parts he was truly excited about. And he made it a priority for us to spend as much time together as possible whenever he was shooting on location. The rest of the year, he was here with me, in Old Pine Cove.

I pulled away from his embrace. "No matter how much I want to keep hugging you, we need to get a move on."

"You're right, let's go."

We got into the car and Justin pulled out of our driveway. "So, have you thought about what we'll tell people when they ask why you can't eat oysters or drink champagne?"

I put my hand on my belly and smiled. "I'll tell them I'm recovering from a nasty stomach bug and the doctor has ordered me to eat super healthy for a couple of weeks. What do you think?"

He nodded. "Yeah, I think people will buy that."

"Besides, everyone will be focusing on you and your Oscar nomination. No one will monitor my food or drink intake. They'll never guess I'm pregnant."

"You're right," he said, glancing at my belly with a loving look in his eyes. "I'm actually happy that this pregnancy is still a secret. I love sharing something with you that no one else is privy to. I'm sure Kermit wouldn't want his mommy to be chased by the paparazzi anyway."

I chuckled. "We talked about this, Justin. We're not naming the baby Kermit."

"Why not? It's a swell name."

I shook my head and beamed at him. "I love you, but Kermit's not a swell baby name. Besides, we can't have a baby and an alpaca with the same name."

He smiled back at me. "I can't believe we're discussing baby names. Remember how you used to hate me for being an immature jerk? What a turn of events. The best ever, of course."

"Well, I'm glad you proved me wrong about being a jerk. I love how you keep making my dreams come true," I said.

"And I will keep making them come true for the rest of our days," he said.

I let out a contented sigh. I had married my dream guy, the inn was doing amazing, and in seven months we would welcome a baby into our home.

Life was absolutely perfect.

NOTE TO MY LOVELY READERS

Thank you so much for reading this book! It means the world to me and I hope you enjoyed it. If you have a minute, I'd be really grateful if you left a review for Love to Prove You Wrong. Reviews help authors more than you might think.

Do you want to receive a free book, updates and the chance to be a part of my ARC team? Subscribe to my newsletter at http://www.sophieleighrobbins.com. I send out newsletters once a week and always keep them concise as I know time is valuable.

Feel free to follow me on social media to get a look behind the scenes, see what I'm up to, check out giveaways or get book recommendations. If you post about my books, make sure to tag me and/or use the hashtag #sophieleighrobbins. I love reposting my readers' pictures!

Acknowledgments

Writing this book has been a blast, but I couldn't have done it without the help and encouragement of a team of amazing people. They all deserve a big thank you!

To my editor Serena Clarke for making my words flow, double-checking facts, and correcting my mistakes. I love working with you!

To my friend and fellow author Kirsty McManus, for reading my words before anyone else, cheering me on, supporting me, and helping me in any way you can: thank you! I'm so lucky to have you in my life.

To all my author friends for offering help, feedback, and encouragement. I love how supportive the romance author/chick lit author community is.

To Brooke, for being there for me, for your kind words, for your help with proofreading, and everything else: thank you so much!

To Vikkie. You are an amazing person and the author community is lucky to have someone like you on their side. Thank you!

To all the bloggers, bookstagrammers, and ARC readers

who spread the news about my books: thank you. It really means a lot to me.

To Ruth, Hilde, Sanne, Malinee, and Liesbeth: I'm honored you love my books so much, but I'm even more honored to be your friend. I love you guys!

To my other friends and my family: thank you for everything.

To Evie, for cheering me on, being on my ARC team, and spreading the word about my books: I appreciate all of it!

To my "Hugo" friends, thank you for the love and support you guys give me with every release.

To Anita Faulkner at Chick Lit & Prosecco. You are such a sweet person, and I can't wait to see your name on your own book soon!

And last but not least, a huge thank you to my husband. You are my favorite adventure and I love you tremendously. Thank you for all that you do.

Also by Sophie-Leigh Robbins

The Best of You

Snowflakes and Sparks (Old Pine Cove #1)

Love to Prove You Wrong (Old Pine Cove #2)

In For a Treat (Old Pine Cove #3)

CPSIA information can be obtained
at www.ICGtesting.com
Printed in the USA
LVHW031433111119
636964LV00001B/140/P